The Devil's Paintbrush

The Devil's Paintbrush

a novel

André Brochu

Translated by
Alison Newall

SIMON & PIERRE FICTION
A MEMBER OF THE DUNDURN GROUP
TORONTO · OXFORD

Copy-editor: Jennifer Bergeron
Design: Jennifer Scott
Printer: Webcom

National Library of Canada Cataloguing in Publication Data

Brochu, André, 1942-
[Épervières. English]
     The devil's paintbrush / André Brochu ; translated by Alison Newall.

Translation of: Les épervières.
ISBN 1-55002-396-9

I. Newall, Alison II. Title. III. Title: Épervières. English.

PS8503.R615E6413 2002   C843'.54   C2002-902133-2   PQ3919.2.B73E7413 2002

1   2   3   4   5   07   06   05   04   03

THE CANADA COUNCIL | LE CONSEIL DES ARTS
FOR THE ARTS | DU CANADA
SINCE 1957 | DEPUIS 1957

Canada

ONTARIO ARTS COUNCIL
CONSEIL DES ARTS DE L'ONTARIO

We acknowledge the support of the **Canada Council for the Arts** and the **Ontario Arts Council** for our publishing program. We also acknowledge the financial support of the **Government of Canada** through the **Book Publishing Industry Development Program** and **The Association for the Export of Canadian Books**, and the Government of Ontario through the **Ontario Book Publishers Tax Credit** program.

Cover Painting: Gustav Klimt, L'arbre de vie, v. 1905–1909

Printed and bound in Canada.❀
Printed on recycled paper.
www.dundurn.com

Dundurn Press
8 Market Street
Suite 200
Toronto, Ontario, Canada
M5E 1M6

Dundurn Press
73 Lime Walk
Headington, Oxford,
England
OX3 7AD

Dundurn Press
2250 Military Road
Tonawanda NY
U.S.A. 14150

Part I

1

Each house is an enigma, sheltering its own impenetrable share of the unknown. It is often an aroma, something about the shadows, the rumour of voices and laughter, songs and shrieks, the rustling of myriad lives. These things, and a thousand other bits of trivia, give each inhabited space its uniqueness. The roofs are imposing or discreet, essentially black with asphalt or tar, but retaining a hint of blue, red, green, or gray. They top masses of brick or wood pierced by windows that open dimly onto pallid interiors, forming watertight containers of life for a few people, sometimes for one, under a tranquil canopy of old trees.

In the houses live beings who are sheltered and free, who attend industriously to the small chores that mark the passing of existence. For it is elsewhere — in offices and factories — that they earn the right to subsist and be happy. Houses are there for the time they have left over, and for pleasure. There, they cook, wash dishes, make love, and raise a few candidates for the future who will, in turn, found their own homes. Houses beget houses, further sanctuaries dedicated to hallowed domestic life, or to selfishness, or to cultivating a couple's delights and hatreds. Houses are nice. They're tidy, redolent of well-tended property. We live and die in houses, there await the passage of time, limpid and eternal. If time stopped passing, stopped short, matter itself would vanish, leaving no trace in memory.

But in some houses — very rare — time stagnates. These are the dwellings of unfettered poverty. They do not elicit sympathetic attention, but simultaneously whet and repel the curiosity of passersby. Dilapidation. Filth. Usually, large families buzz about them, and sometimes they turn pretty spots, adorned with trees and water, into dumps. The Tourangeau house is like that. Blue, enormous, and hunched, it rises up halfway down the slope between the road and the water.

The river. At the foot of the lot, its current rises in a vast movement that, a little further along, turns back on itself, forming a large eddy. Lucie Tourangeau is quite proud of this whirlpool. She has nothing, yet the blessing of this reversing current is hers. Across the river, on Île Jésus, she glimpses mansions hidden in the greenery, lawns rushing down to the lapping rapids, and tells herself that, over there, the water flows in the orthodox direction, from southwest to northwest. The rich people across the way might envy her current.

There is also the drop-off, twenty-five metres deep, just off shore. It is deep enough to hold several houses piled atop each other. When she swims, Lucie Tourangeau pauses, upright, just above the abyss, and listens from within her own depths to the silence below. She communes through flesh and blood with the stony river bottom, urinates languorously into the dark water, and is fulfilled.

There is this bounty, and the public's bounty: Lucie Tourangeau is a well-cared-for pauper. Swimming against the currents of fashion and comfort, she has no trouble feeding and clothing her nine children, endowing them an old-fashioned look in modern times, a distinguished air, overflowing with health — and great drive, too. They have a way of venturing freely out into peaceful territory, of confounding decorum. In spite of the public's solicitude, the Tourangeaus are a feared tribe. Nice, of course! Well spoken — speech marred by carelessness, yet sprinkled with rare expressions springing up about the edges, manners that abruptly reveal indications of a proper upbringing — and then an utter, profound, spontaneous, incurable lack of distinction, inherited from their mother: La Lucie, whose name alone can make her peaceful neighbours sigh.

Sigh — that gangling beanpole, Dutch on her father's side, Mohawk on her mother's, that monument of pregnancies whose ideas are enough to make you laugh and grind your teeth, such a fright in her big rumpled dresses!

She lives with her string of boys and girls in a two-dwelling house by the water. The house must have been charming, once, beneath its fifty-year-old ash trees. No more. Among them, the ten occupants quickly transformed it to suit themselves. Three years ago, they acquired this un-hoped-for lodging following a joint intervention by the mayor and the parish priest, and marked the event with various gestures of appropriation that have left spectacular traces. The front yard particularly is choked with debris of all types and sizes: unhinged bedroom doors, scattered shutters, old windows whose panes were shattered by the violent child, Fernand, and which have now been replaced by plywood. Not to mention the harvest of imported booty —

tires, hubcaps, and road signs, collected during enthusiastic escapades — that has become a permanent feature of the domestic landscape. The property soon earned the unenviable label of "pigsty," bestowed by a unanimous neighbourhood, and the value of adjacent properties plunged dramatically. To add to the disgrace, the sewage pipes and septic tank proved inadequate, and so an open stream now runs toward the river, scattering germs and odours in all directions. When wind stirs, discerning neighbourhood noses complain, "It smells like the Tourangeaus!" La Lucie has conscientiously notified the City, but her impecuniosity shelters her from quick action.

All in all, Lucie is a nice woman, courageous, kind, generous, and even beautiful, in spite of the menace of rapid decline common to the Amerindians. But you can see why her husband, a bohemian himself, stuck her there and went to live in the city in his studio on Rue Saint-Paul, where he makes enormous plush animals, each one more fantastical than the last. There, he consoles himself for having been ousted by his crop of offspring from first place in her affections. From a distance, he still considers her the queen of his heart — she who, until recently, kept peopling the world with new beings drawn from her entrails as if the act of giving birth was her life's purpose.

She's had seven children, all handsome and full of life, though sometimes a little short on health, despite appearances. This gives rise to vigorous illnesses: double pneumonias and very scarlet fevers that bring their victim to death's door. Then three days after the priest has come, the dying one is splashing in puddles once again.

Seven children. But when the people across the street moved without leaving a forwarding address, or anything but two starving brats, Lucie, heeding only her heart and her passion for children, added them to her brood on the spot: a little girl and a wee rascal, adorably enchanting. Lucie has vowed to fatten them up and pamper them until she has erased all memory of their former existence as child martyrs. Tiny compared to their new brothers and sisters, Corinne and Stéphane exert remarkable yet subtle authority over them and are taking them great strides forward in vice and duplicity.

One afternoon, using a furtive scenario invented by Stéphane, Fernand (the violent one) and Bernadette (the youngest) secretly absconded with the magic jars that Lucie stores in her huge bedroom cupboard for use in her presentations. The containers hold fetuses at various stages of development. The Tourangeau children would never have dreamed of stealing such maternal treasures for their own amusement. Although you have to admit that in this case they had considerable entertainment potential. The halted lives, wedged into their glass prisons, almost lay bare the soul itself, which seems at one with the slender fingers jointed like a spider's legs, and especially with the alien faces that appear to ponder the inconsequentiality of human decisions. Lucie uses them to explain that Life is preferable to all else, and that poverty — of which she is a shining example — cannot justify the slaughter of innocents in which modern savagery indulges. She has been a militant member of the pro-life movement for two years, finding in it a powerful means of self-actualization, as well as a chance to escape from the daily round of chores once in a while. Outside her immediate circle — they would never take her seriously, since nobody is a prophet in their own country — a natural inclination for humanitarian action allows her to exercise her apostolic mission, replete with high-sounding words and moving gestures. The little bundles of waterlogged flesh, suspended in formaldehyde, are always a tremendous success, especially with children, whose juicy questions often relate to their cartoon heroes. The contemporary imagination makes good use of intra-uterine esthetics in its depiction of typical physiognomy.

Arms loaded with the precious jars, Fernand and Babette (the youngest's nickname) hug the wall of the house beside the hedge and take refuge in the old garbage pit, now bristling with devil's paintbrush. Stéphane and Corinne await them there. Fernand stipulates that they have to be careful not to break any of the jars. That would be a catastrophe. They'll just look and pretend to be abortionists and not touch anything. Lucie has told her children about the horrors of this diabolical action, hoping to instill a sound respect for life. Stéphane, having invented the game and cast the roles, will play the fetus. He sits down between Babette's legs. She is younger, but just as tall and twice as heavy — a five-year-old giant. It is Fernand's job to *extract* him, using a piece of garden hose as a siphon. Corinne plays the nurse. The sequence of actions to be performed seems complete, and now they're eager to carry them out. Fernand clowns noisily, proud of his executioner's role. The sturdy boy dislikes Stéphane, despises his intelligence and skill — weapons of the weak! Subconsciously, he is mainly resentful of the place Stéphane and his sister have usurped in his mother's heart. The play-acting will let him get back on top, and, in his imagination, eliminate a secret rival.

"Shut up, Fernand! You're going to get us get caught!" says Corinne. "Stop fooling around and be the doctor. I'm going to pass you the siphon. Are you guys ready?"

Babette growls yes. In spite of her age, the little girl can barely talk. Usually, she just sniggers or makes sounds that have no specific meaning. Stéphane's head on her belly makes her giggle. She knows she's the mother, and this huge baby is going to be sucked out of her through a little tube. It isn't real, but it's really funny.

"Okay," says Fernand. "Let's get started. Nurse Corinne, the siphon please."

"Yes, doctor."

Corinne passes the green plastic serpent to Fernand and, at first, he doesn't know what to do with it. Then he stretches one end toward a jar and presses the other against Stéphane's belly button. Stéphane shudders at the touch, then stiffens, seeming to gather himself up. He becomes even smaller and makes a strange hissing noise as he slowly starts to emerge from between Babette's legs. Babette shakes with laughter as he makes his way toward the sun-flooded jars.

"He looks like a pickle!" says Fernand. Faced with this hilarious spectacle, he can't stay in character.

"Shut up!" Corinne protests. "You're going to wreck everything."

Stéphane inches toward the jars with small movements of feet and buttocks, still wearing the sorrowful expression he's had since he starting playing the part of the evicted child. But then he stops, exclaiming, "Darn! We've got to start over. I forgot the most important thing."

"What?"

"When you're taking a baby out, it doesn't just come. It's got to fight, make a fuss."

Corinne, who understands, bursts out laughing. Fernand and Babette laugh too, a little late.

"We're starting over. You, Babette, squeeze me a little with your legs like you don't want to let me go. Hey! Not so hard, you bloody savage! You're smothering me! Doctor, you stay in character or I'll make you eat those pickles."

Any outside observer would find this David-to-Goliath threat a little strange.

They start over. With his head on the girl's belly, Stéphane twists around for a good spell as if he's being torn in different directions while his pretend mother chortles with glee. Excited, Fernand dances in front of the two, so entranced that he ends up wetting his pants. When he realizes what has happened, he bursts into laughter.

"Hey! I peed my pants!"

The others abandon the game instantly, seized with noisy hilarity. Fernand is delighted to be the centre of attention. He wrings the wet cloth with his hands, miming grotesque gestures and parading his enjoyment. Then, suspecting a mocking undertone, his mood suddenly changes and, furious, he sends the jars flying away with great kicks. One jar breaks, rolling its contents into the grass.

This, of course, puts an end to the fun. Alerted by their

yells, Lucie descends on them. She is as upset as if she'd lost a child, and, with a loud display of despair, even raises her hand to Fernand, who fends her off with a spectacular tantrum. Stéphane and Corinne — easily overlooked among the others, and especially indulged by their adoptive mother — grow quieter than ever and produce the demure smiles of well-behaved children. Fernand denounces them, but in vain. Everyone is against him, and he gives way to wracking sobs.

Lucie is completely beside herself. She runs out to buy a padlock before the stores close, determined that, from now on, her precious jars will be kept safe from such profane curiosity. When she gets back, though, she is plagued by a fear of losing the key. She is unused to these tiny metal contrivances — for Lucie, the best guarantee of happiness is a house that is open to all comers — so she decides to leave the key on her night table and vows to check regularly to make sure it's still there.

2

A few days have gone by.

One hot morning — a July morning in 1983, with the thermometer already hitting twenty-five Celsius — Étienne, the oldest boy, wakes up on the wrong side of the bed. The dense light of day shines through the uncurtained window. It should imbue him with the young summer's ardour, give him confidence, but confidence is sulking, draped in poverty. Everything is asleep around him. Gervais sprawls next to him, naked, snoring innocently within a swarm of dreams. At sixteen, his carrot-top and illusory femininity make him a charming rascal, ambiguously elfin, all sparks and sputters like a striking match. Étienne has often yielded to his pestering caresses, just for the fun of it, for the clash of flesh, the whetting of desire. This morning, though, faced with a body pulsing like a heart under the day's hot fist, he muses bitterly about an impossible purity, about a life of poverty that must be content with present pleasures, and deny the future.

The future … Étienne is eighteen, and he wants to earn a living, but how? How? First he'd have to make La Lucie listen to reason, but every time he talks about finding a job, she hangs all over him, talking him out of it, infusing his whole body with the sweet poison of heedlessness, holding him to her like a liege knight. She croons that things are fine as they are, that if he has an income, she won't be able to get welfare, and then where would they be? Always the same song, the same sweet song full of words that lament and caress. Her large eyes gazing into his, a mother's eyes, immensely brown, like a fool's paradise. He gets lost in them: he's never been able to stand fast in the face of such concern. What does she get out of keeping them close, tied to her apron strings, these males who are hollow under their blooming complexions and rampant females?

One day, he'll have to make the break, take off, even if it means crashing later. After all, his own father fled this enervating sweetness, this song full of milk and honey. Oh, to go there, stay under his wing … Right! Well, you don't leave one nest for another, and, besides, Étienne isn't sure it would be any better.

His father, what a puppet! Behind his rebellions, his hard, rejecting face, his small soul flutters like a butterfly, always ready to run. The village called him Chonchon when he was a little boy, and the name has stuck. Étienne always shudders when he hears it, as though he has a lace and papier mâché father instead of the usual big brute his schoolmates complained about. A flamboyant father, a poet, and, what's more, a drunk, who makes plush fantasies for the well-tended offspring of the ascendant class. Every year, there's a story in the papers about this original craftsman and his astounding imagination. "Chimeras by Chonchon." The magician's own children never had their solitude enlivened by one of these cozy monsters whose ugliness was so charming. At home, the magician showed only his coward's face.

Étienne looks about, surrounded by a familiar mess. Everything is tossed higgledy-piggledy: clothes, shoes, faded comics reread a hundred times, dirty dishes in the wildest array of shapes and colours, despairing of one day finding their way to the sink. It is all incredibly dirty, as if the dust that has accumulated over three years is blending with the fabric, the objects, imbuing them with its colloidal qualities. Étienne's eyes wander over the general greyness, which is sharply highlighted by the sun in spite of the dirty windows, and he plunges into sadness, quickly overwhelmed by the sense of his own impotence. What can he do in the face of an entire household's smiling, unconscious unwillingness?

He gets up, looks around in vain for clean underwear, and pulls on his jeans and a T-shirt. He turns back to the bed where Gervais still lies snoring and, with a sort of tenderness, draws the sheet up over the proffered body. Everything's out in the open in this house, he thinks, without pushing the idea any further, although it settles into him, beneath awareness. It is the shape of his despair. In the open. Exposed to the fine rain of debris from the air, the world, perhaps the stars, and treading in the dust of a decomposing destiny, entropy, a vast cosmic collapse. Étienne treads in a universal despondency. He sees his youngest brothers in a pile, drunk with sleep and base dreams. He notices the girls' crude beauty, garnished with long red or ebony hair, bouquets of grace destined for inevitable despoiling. He, too, is destined for it, like a girl, but without the pleasure. Life will crush his meagre hopes one by one, until he regrets he was ever born.

No! He shakes himself. No! He'll stand up, rise above all this, above failure. He'll stare sweet, foolish Lucie in the eye, his big, filthy mother with her vague dreams. He'll ball up his fists, won't think twice about using them to clear his path to freedom, to where tenderness, strength, even ambition can blossom. He will be great, he will be the one to take his place among men, earn a full measure of honour and respect like a priceless tribute. Étienne! He will be Étienne Tourangeau, the one who pulled himself out of the family quagmire, out of poverty, sheer folly and insignificance, who hauled himself all the way to ... Shit! He's eighteen and he hasn't done a thing yet, nothing, he has no education, not a penny to his name, isn't even blessed with the amorality that would let him make some quick cash by selling scintillating death — coke, crack, heroin. Becoming successful while keeping your hands clean when everything has been against you from your birth: quite the challenge!

The laundry is piled right up to the stairs that connect the two apartments. The house is sagging under the weight of all these rags, the clothes which the village first strutted in, then happily got rid of, glad to have a way of proving its benevolence. Consignments are sometimes so large that La Lucie stops doing laundry: there's always something clean to wear. You just have to hunt for it, which can take a while since, here, nothing is ever wasted. There are no garbage cans in this part of the world, the final destination for tattered elegance.

Étienne goes down the stairs, shoving piles of clothes aside with his foot. The two apartments are completely separate, and he has to go outdoors to get to the ground floor. He pushes open the never-locked door. Here, too, chaos greets him. He tries to imagine what the room would look like without all this clutter. Two or three days a year, at holiday time, the mounds of charity are moved into a bedroom, and the living room abounds with balloons, tinsel, garish ornaments arranged according to each one's taste. Fantastic outfits are assembled from the parish linen, adding a crowning touch to the ambience of total hysteria.

"She's fine here, with all this," he thinks. "She" is La Lucie, whom he loves and fears and despises simultaneously, pities and would like to protect from the touch of folly that is the source of her misfortunes, and those of all around her. But how do you talk sense into your mother? He'd rather collapse onto her shoulder and melt, dissolve into tears, into scalding words, stammer out his great unhappiness, take refuge in her warmth and sweetness, hear her voice pour over him like the patter of rain, her large mothering body sheltering him from his sorrow, protecting him from his fractured present, absolving him from regret and hatred, strengthening him against the revulsion that courses through him and spoils his life.

Mom, he'd say, why are we in this shit? How come we don't live like normal people, have a normal chance to get what we want, tenderness, beauty, wealth even? Why are we always at the bottom of the heap? What keeps us trapped in this ugliness, this despair? His head would be on her shoulder, and she'd stroke him gently, silently, and his questions would turn into a single moan, a solitary sound. And then she would murmur the secret, ancient, savage words learned from her mother, words whose meaning she has forgotten, that tie a knot in memory, words that fend off how bad everything seems, the malice of circumstance and destiny. She'd soothe him, her large hand running over the small of his back, uniting the fragmented distresses of a now adult body that doesn't know where to turn, so turns to her, the mother, the faith, the filth.

Lucie's bedroom is next to the kitchen, and she sleeps with her door open so she can keep an eye on things. As soon as Étienne steps into the large sun-filled room, she calls to him in a low voice, "Étienne, what time is it, darling?"

"Ten to seven," he says, checking the clock.

"Good God, are you ever up early this morning! What's going on? Are you sick?"

"Of course not! A little insomnia, that's all."

"Is something wrong?"

"Anyway, everybody gets up now, Mom. It's not insomnia when you get up at the same time as everybody else."

"You're the one who said insomnia. Come, come over here."

In the middle of the large bed, with only her head showing above the taut sheet, she presents a rare picture, free of the litter of objects with which she is always surrounded. The bed is a desert, and she is buried beneath the white sands. Framed by long, tousled hair, her face looks like a mask of the moon; she is a moon that speaks, her voice emerging from beneath the sand, barely audible because she doesn't want to wake the children, who are asleep in the next room.

Étienne knows she is naked under the sheet. He keeps himself from imagining the body that, when he was little, she displayed openly, innocently and often, to all eyes.

He stands nearby, and she gazes at him with a wide smile, doubtless proud of the fine specimen of young manhood she brought into the world. Étienne lets her admire him, then sinks back into his gloom. He has to keep his problems, his dissatisfaction to himself — she has powerful arguments to set against any faltering steps toward liberation. "You don't look happy," she begins, reaching to him over the sheet that shrouds her. The great smooth beach that is the bed is now somewhat misshapen, collapsing in places, affording glimpses of the figure extending from the head, belying its lunar solitude. She is an ocean, a tide that surges well beyond the confines of the bed, filling the room, the whole house with her soft, warm presence, overflowing into the yard in miscellaneous heaps; she is Lucie, radiance and fanatical love spread around her, matching the huge brown eyes that conceal nothing of her soul. She is a soul, an utterly radiant body, a torrent of flesh proffered in sacrifice for the children who are an extension of her, for Étienne, who does not know what to do with this gift.

All this tenderness irritates him, and he falls back on practical issues.

"Do you need me today?"

"No, sweetheart. Do you want to go out?"

"Yes. I need to do something."

"Going to see the girls?" she titters.

This is a maternal tack that Étienne can't stand, when she starts touching on his few private attachments and desires. He rebels.

"A guy like me doesn't have much to do with girls. I've got no job. I've got no money to take them out with, out to eat, to the movies. I don't have a single thing that girls want from a guy. I'd be better off as a fag."

"Oh, come on, the girls will find out about you fast enough. A cute guy like you has nothing to worry about. You think that's all that matters to them, money?"

She strokes his thigh lightly, with the tips of her fingers. He steps back.

"Is there anything for breakfast?"

"Of course, darling. When have I ever let you go without? There's always food in the house. Try not to wake up the little ones; I'd like to get some more sleep."

She must have had to spend part of the night fornicating with one of her men. They turn up at around eleven o'clock, when the youngest children, who sleep downstairs, are in bed. The visitors stay closeted with her until two or three in the morning. Since she had her big operation, she no longer worries about nasty surprises and submits to the claims of nature without displeasure. The men she accommodates don't find fault with her ways or the dishevelled look of the house.

They sometimes give her a hefty slap, or a fifty-dollar bill, depending how they feel. Étienne isn't jealous of them anymore, no longer spies on them to see how they behave. He has benefited from the ruling regime of charity, and is only surprised that his sisters, the oldest of whom are fourteen and fifteen, have not — as far as he knows — begun to ply a munificent public with their charms.

He gulps down three slices of toast and a cup of bad coffee, then counts his money and dashes blithely out of the house. In spite of the heat, the morning's air, ruffled by a light breeze, is breathable; the piping of bluebirds, accompanied by the blackbirds' grating call, introduces a subtle gaiety. Étienne barely notices the rubbish strewn around the yard. Leaving his mother and his misery behind him, he recaptures the fleeting but violent joy that always attends his departures, when renewal and freedom could still await him at the end of the road and he hasn't been seized by the suffocating thought of his destiny.

3

"Oh, you little pig!"

Lucie has just caught sight of Bernadette, the youngest, her cherished Babette. A long green string runs from Babette's nose, and the rest of her face is unevenly spattered with dirt and jam. The spectacle moves her, calling forth a full complement of indulgence.

"Come here and let me clean you up a little." She grabs the dishcloth and chases her daughter, who is terrified of the abuse inflicted by clean water.

"A pretty little thing like you can't go around all covered in dirt! What would people say?"

She's got her now and forces the rag's smelly caress on her. Babette shrieks as if she's being murdered, pummelling her mother with fists and feet, calming down as soon as the assault is over.

"Honey, why are you hurting mummy? Don't you like being clean? You're so pretty when you're clean."

"Don't want to be pretty!" mumbles the child, her voice forced, sputtering like a string of hiccups.

"Come on, a little beauty like you! What would the Good Lord say? You know, not every girl has the good fortune to be a beauty. Would you rather look like a witch, with hair like a grey mop, a crooked nose, pointy teeth, and a face that's all red and bumpy?"

"Yes!" announces Babette with a bold, mischievous laugh.

Fernand has just stepped into the kitchen and he laughs, too, exclaiming, "Babette, you don't have to turn into a witch, 'cause you already are one! You're a real fart face!"

Mother and daughter howl in protest, and Fernand roars with joy.

"You, you're a mental case, Fernand," Babette sputters back, finally.

"If you ever say that again, I'll strangle you!" Suddenly serious, the boy starts to carry out his threat.

"Mom, Mom! He's hurting me! Let me go, you goddamn f …"

"Fernand! Let go of your sister, right now!"

"She's got to apologize first! Say you're sorry, Babette, or I'll kill you! Say it!"

"So … sorry …"

"Louder!"

"Sorry!"

Fernand lets her go, her face crimson with suffocation and rage.

"Mental case, mental case!" taunts the child from the safety of her mother's arms.

"Mom! Tell her to stop or I don't know what I'll do to her!"

"Calm down, both of you! I've never seen anything like it! Are you Catholics or little heathen? What would Baby Jesus say?"

"Mom, Baby Jesus doesn't exist."

"What! What did you say?"

Fernand is gazing at her with that triumphant look he gets when he happens upon an idea that's beyond his years.

"God's just a bunch of lies they used to tell in the old days to keep the kids quiet. Like Santa Claus."

"Fernand! Do you know what you're saying?"

"Out of the mouth of babes," says a placid voice that has a metallic ring to it.

"Father Lanthier!" The screen door frames the cleric's plump silhouette. Instantly reconciled, Fernand and Babette duck out through the living room, and Lucie, disconcerted, splutters a string of vague apologies as she collects herself and hurries forward. "Come in, come in, Father! What a lovely surprise! You should have come to the front door."

"I wanted to see the banks of your pretty river once more. And, of course, I love to surprise my parishioners, see them the way they are naturally."

"The way they are! You can say that again, Father. If I'd known you were coming, I would have dressed up a little, done my hair … You're always doing us such good!"

"Well, exactly! I didn't want to put you to all that trouble. After all, the Good Lord always sees you exactly as you are. Why should his priest have any extra privileges? The Church, you know, Lucie, has changed a great deal since Vatican II. It's closer to the people now. All that pretense is over with! It is the soul that matters to the Church." His voice sounds somewhat weary, with a hint of irony moderating his position's mandatory inflexibility. He seems to live by rote, driven by a duty that time has adapted to fit any situation. "Little Fernand is giving you a catechism lesson?" he continues, feigning detachment.

"Oh, Father, that one is going to drive me crazy! Can you tell me where he gets those twisted ideas, which he trots out just to make us angry?"

The priest appears to ponder for a moment, then directs a cold stare at her. "Upon my word, my good woman, I think I know. In fact, that's one of the things I wanted to talk to you about."

A little anxious, she keeps her gaze steady as he draws out an adroit pause. He opens his mouth just as she's about to speak. "Sometimes, my dear Lucie, acts of charity can lead to precisely the opposite of what you'd be entitled to expect. If you'll permit me to indulge in an analogy in the style of the great Lafontaine, if a mother dog brings two wolf cubs into her litter, even though she treats them just like her own puppies, one day she'll be surprised and grieved to discover that not only are the two little adoptees actually wolves, but they've also had a bad influence on her children. There, I think that's perfectly clear."

Stunned by these brutal words, Lucie is at first speechless, then a gnawing anger begins to rise within her. This isn't the first time the priest has voiced such observations, but this time he's gone too far. With her most generous instincts under attack, she turns suddenly, like a cornered animal. "Do you mean to say, Father, that I shouldn't have taken in those two children, children who were abandoned heartlessly, who suffered torture at the hands of their parents? Do you mean to say that I should have let them go to foster homes, where things could have been even worse? Aren't you happy, Father, that these children now have a decent home, a home that has taken them in with love and not for money?"

"My dear woman, when it comes to charity, I believe I know a bit more about it than you do."

Seeing her protector's vexed demeanour, Lucie opts to defuse the discussion with her most inane titter. "Father, of course I didn't mean to lecture you!"

"I am fully aware — perhaps, you will agree, more so than you are, since I am a priest — of our sacred duty to help our neighbours. However, while generosity is perfectly praiseworthy in and of itself, it shouldn't blind a benefactor to the risks it can entail."

"But really, Father! Children! Seven and eight years old! They don't even know what sin is yet."

"My dear Lucie, you'd be surprised to know how much iniquity and filth can be lurking behind those angelic faces. These little ones were born and raised in vice. Certainly, they aren't responsible for the seeds of sin that were planted in them, but they're dangerous nonetheless, just like a rotten apple that, carelessly left in a barrelful of good ones, quickly spoils them all!"

"I beg your pardon, Father! You've been here for five minutes and I haven't even offered you a seat. There's the rocking chair, you like that one. Just a second and I'll clear it off." The chair is covered with crumpled clothing, and she carries the pile into the next room. The diversion does not fool the priest, and he sits down, resigned. "It's already quite warm out. What can I get you? I've got some nice cold lemonade. Here, let me take your hat."

"No, thank you, I'll just hold it. But lemonade now, some lemonade would be nice."

"Right away, Father."

His hat, a panama, lies on his knees. He can't bring himself to put it down anywhere. Everything is so messy that the hat might get sullied, or even infested with vermin.

"Here you go, Father. It's really quite hot out today." The priest takes the glass, holding it by his fingertips as if he were afraid of getting dirty. He looks at it despondently, then deposits it on a nearby buffet. "Don't you like it, Father?"

"I'm not thirsty anymore. My dear Lucie, I've come this morning —" He breaks off, appearing to examine his thoughts, organizing them the way he does when he is about to give a sermon. When he continues, his tone is as even as a mechanism that will drone on until it reaches the end of its wooden lament. "— to inform you of how dissatisfied — the word is not too strong — some people are with you. This is nothing new. When you were living in the village, I often had to act as your neighbours' spokesman, tell you about their observations and even their complaints, which, by the way, were completely justified. I thought, however, that moving you here would make a difference. Moreover, you solemnly promised that you would mend your ways and do everything you could to make your generous benefactors happy, particularly the mayor, since I myself seem to have little influence over your decisions."

"Father!" objects Lucie, fixing him with her large, limpid eyes. "How can you say that!"

"Please, don't interrupt. I have a lot to say, and I want to get through it. Where should I begin? Oh, yes! The mayor, my good

Lucie, is very disappointed. When he arranged for you to get this house by the water, a dream house, the perfect place to raise your children in peace, safe from bad influences — you know what I mean — he thought that you would maintain the place, if only out of gratitude, and maybe even improve it by taking care of the yard, putting in flower beds, that kind of thing. It's clear that gardening is not your strong suit, but, like the mayor, I'm appalled at the fact that your lawn has become a wasteland of weeds and hay, and worst of all, that the yard is now a veritable garbage dump. That's not too strong a word …"

For the first few moments, Lucie attends to his remonstrances, but she slowly starts to daydream, though she pretends to listen deferentially to the priest. The pale hat on his knees distracts her, it is such a contrast to his dark garb — black pants and jacket, a deep purple shirt that reminds her of Good Friday. How can anyone brave summer like that, wearing night's attire, with the heat of day blasting out like a furnace? Poor man! He must be really hot! She would like to take him into her room, undo his buttons one by one. His chest would peep whitely through his greying hair, then his belly button, a tiny baptismal font. Then she would undo his belt, and his pants would fall to his ankles, and she would uncover him completely, lay him bare, and he would let her, like a child. She would lay him on his back and, with the powerful femaleness that radiates from her bobbing nipples, her consuming abyss, she would transform this chubby fifty year old into a turgid, steaming prayer, perform the ritual sacrifice to the gods of pleasure. She would make this venom-filled preacher a happy man, ecstasy bubbling from his lips like milk.

Sated, replete. He would hum, wearied, in a ravished, prone stupor. A true priest, purged by her expert care, as gentle and humble as an old-fashioned choirboy embarrassed by his robes.

"Are you listening, my child?"

"Yes, yes, Father, but …"

"You'll have your turn to speak, if you think there's anything to say. I'm simply passing along the mayor's warning. The complaints he's received are very serious; I hope you understand that."

"Well, complaints …"

"Thoroughly justified complaints. Do you know what's stopping some of your neighbours from putting their houses up for sale? For one thing, their value has dropped so much that they can't bring themselves to take such a disastrous step. For another, they don't know what kind of people would want to buy a house in such a rundown neighbourhood. Then there's the risk of disreputable purchasers jumping on the opportunity to buy cheap and running their properties down as well … The waterfront, the pride of the community, would become a disgrace, and whose fault would that be? Yours!" His reddening jowls tremble slightly below finely wrought white metal glasses. Lucie likes his anger, which warms his skin with feeling. "Do you understand? The church council and the town unite to get you out of trouble, and all you do is turn the home they gave you into a sty!"

"Father! If I could just say something?"

"I know what you're going to say, so don't bother. And I have lots more …"

"Forgive me for insisting, Father, but you know quite well

that I was moved here by force after being essentially thrown out of the house in the village, where my children and I were very comfortable. The house that was owned by my father-in-law, and which therefore belonged to my husband's family."

"That's precisely the problem, my dear woman! You make yourselves unwelcome everywhere, you and your badly brought up tribe. You realize that we — the town — have ways of getting rid of you, do you hear me? To banish you if you don't change your attitude and refuse to behave in a civilized manner!"

Stunned, Lucie stares at this bald, well-fed man whose eyes are as round as his glasses. He's used a strong word — banish, banish — he's threatening to send her to the devil, she who has, who should have some rights to this land in this country. All of a sudden, she realizes that the era of tolerance has ended, that the vague pity and affection that have always surrounded and protected her — probably because of her widely respected father-in-law — have evaporated. For a long time, the old doctor's mantle lay over his descendants, over Chonchon especially, the youngest, who was forgiven for his bohemian ways, for having married such an unlikely girl. But now that has gone, and she'll have to play hardball.

"Doctor Tourangeau," she says, to verify her disgrace, "always told me that I could rely on my neighbours' benevolence, when … He knew that Chonchon wouldn't be able to support me and …"

"You should realize that that's over with; it's in the past. The good doctor has been gone for several years, and it's useless to depend on his influence. He is remembered as a perfectly honest man, and people deplore the fact that his descendants are so unlike him. One look at you, at your home, at your badly dressed children, and it's obvious that you are nothing like him, nothing at all!"

Shaken by these words, Lucie bursts into tears. "But Father, that man loved me. If it wasn't for him, I would have left my husband and all the children he kept giving me. He told me that I was indispensable to them. He accepted my habits, my way of seeing things. He said that love was the most important thing, and he knew that, in spite of my shortcomings, Father, none of my children would ever go without and, most of all, they would always have the love that makes life possible."

"Love is good, of course. I preach it every Sunday! But do you think it's enough?"

Lucie is sobbing now. Broken, she collapses at his feet. She wraps her arms around his knees, her mumbled words half drowned in grief. He remains still, waiting for the crisis to pass, but still she holds on, and, little by little, becomes increasingly insistent. He becomes frantic as it dawns on him that he has fallen into a trap of foul affection, that this crying woman is capable of anything. He wants to get up, run away, but she is stronger than he is, and his resistance suddenly gives way to her infectious madness. He pales, his head spinning, and loses all sense of reality. For a second, he retains an instinct to fight, resist the terrible pleasure being offered to him, push off the hands that are so expert at gentle, efficient, motherly care. Then he yields, consents, lets himself be overwhelmed by the tender, smothering wave, suddenly finds himself in a large, moon-like bed, where life, with long arms and immense breasts, envelops his desire. Now it's clear, and he, the priest, lies naked beneath her as she thrashes like a hundred demons, watching him, and he wants to lick her smile full of large, slightly yellow teeth. Her large brown eyes have no depth, yet are filled with foolish dreams, and they bewitch him bit by bit, with little shocks of boundless joy drawn from some unknown source, as if this miserable existence could secrete something other than misfortune and death. How smooth, like silk, this stomach against his own, this sharing of heat. And now he communes with the joy that seizes him, or the pleasure, since this is a base affair of flesh, of animal, almost vegetal rhythms, a vast rush of blood and juice, an utter distension — ecstasy!

4

Walking along with his pockets full of time, Étienne often thinks about God. He watches himself advance as if he were two people. He sees himself, advancing alone because the fact that he's a Tourangeau, the son of crazy Lucie, sets him apart and makes him someone who can be greeted but not befriended. He pictures himself moving along the roads, penetrating the heavens, which close behind him with a rustling of leaves and a swishing of clouds. And he thinks about God. His mother often talks about God, although she's not devout. She's pious by nature and treats her creator with more love than respect. Étienne is the same. He has turned God into someone to talk to during his long walks. With the feeling of his legs beating out the pace, his body vibrating with each step, his penis floating in his jeans, the belt pulled tight around his stomach, his limbs stretching freely, a rhythm of prayer overtakes him.

At first, he murmurs silently, without thinking: God, God, my God. Then more words come: great God, great, high, and holy, my high and holy God in heaven, heaven, and now, because of this presence, he sees the heavens better. The sky is like a beast's quivering snout, radiant with blue and white air cells that are also distances, rays in which the being without form exists, greater than all else because it contains everything, the means by which I, Étienne, exist. And Étienne feels proud, and, happy, he evades his pathetic outlook, his lot as a boy with no trade, no place in world. Now he's not a child: he's a man filled with the joy of living, and the joy transforms him. He is reborn; rather, he is born all new into his skin, minute by minute, into the clothes that share his nakedness like a second skin. He feels handsome, young, and pure. God streaks through him like a comet's tail.

Houses then become benevolent accidents, heaven's acolytes lining his path. He moves forward amidst bounty and blessings. Behind a window that reflects daylight like a ghost, sometimes he catches a glimpse of an old woman's ivory head as she watches him pass, unafraid of being seen. There are such old women whose only job seems to be watching, like witnesses, everything that passes by, young and old, good and bad, the unusual, the unexpected. A tease, Étienne waves and sometimes throws them a kiss or an obscene gesture, depending how he feels. They never turn a hair, but their icy judgments will add to the weight of evidence continually being amassed against the family of vagabonds in the court of public opinion, the vagabonds sprung from the good doctor's work like a punishment for some nameless crime. Étienne feels nearly happy, almost proud to belong to the race of wolves, to receive his life's vocation straight from heaven, where a great, holy, gentle God loves him wholeheartedly, unconditionally, loves even his hunger and his occasional shame, his deep yearning for freedom. Ah! the air, the air before his eyes fills him with a serene hope, tinted blue.

When he gets to the viaduct that straddles the rapids, where the lake pours into the river, Étienne stops to ponder what to do with his day. He could go to one of the islands, hopping across the stones, and fish using the rudimentary tackle he's got hidden in the bush. If he's lucky he could catch a bass or pike. But he doesn't have a fishing licence, and it would be hard to sell the fish. Potential buyers have been aware of pollution's effects for a quite a while now, and they are wary: "A nice pike, ma'am?" "No, sir! Your fish is pretty fishy!" In ecology, wordplay often replaces logic.

He has another idea: he could go over to Laval West and make some money on the golf course. Then he could catch a train to Montreal. To do that, he'll have to use the train bridge. That makes him a little nervous, has ever since the accident a few years back when Ti-Nest Laroche got killed that way. The urchin hadn't counted on the express train coming through and he was out in the middle when the train started onto the bridge. The jolting of the metal structure he was clinging to made him lose his grip, and he smashed his head on the rocks that protruded from the current's web. The current was strong just there, and his body was fished out well downstream.

Étienne makes sure no train is coming by putting his palm on the steel rails, which still hold night's coolness. He even puts his ear to them, like a Plains Indian would have done. If anybody's watching, what will they think I'm doing! He gives the finger to potential spectators and stands up, satisfied. Then, with a vigorous stride, he starts onto the tracks, taking two ties with each step. It's clear sailing — no railway workers are around and the station is out of sight. At the bridge, he gazes down at the boiling water beneath him. Then, trusting his Indian genes to protect him from vertigo, he ventures onto the bridge. But now he doesn't skip ties. He moves with mincing steps that make him look like a clown or a queer. In spite of all his precautions, he doesn't feel safe: a train could have been stopped at the station while he was checking the rails. The fear just grazes him; he's not the kind of boy to be scared for no reason, especially now that he's past the age of childish terrors. The time for complacent shivers is over, and that's too bad, since fear added spice to the adventure. Now, he's left with only the satisfaction of tearing himself away from what he loves and which demeans him.

In the middle of the bridge, Étienne pauses to watch the spectacle of black and foaming water, the eddies assaulting the rocks and being sucked under by the current. The drop in the riverbed is so great that during the summer the liquid mass gets concentrated in a relatively narrow passage, unleashing all the demons of the element. The sky around him is now very blue. He stands above the void and, like his mother when she swims above the abyss, he feels the need to empty himself, to commune with the economy of water. He liberates his penis and empties his bladder, while the gulls circle in the July sun. Now, lighter, he starts toward the shore once more, wholly recovered from his painful awakening in that hot, dirty house, as if he had bathed in the frigid waves.

Nearing the golf course, which is bounded by high cedars whose fragrance, in the dense shadow, evokes holidays and forests, Étienne recalls the summers during his childhood when he hired himself out as a caddie. Back then, the trains came more often, and conductors shut their eyes to the bunch of rascals who crowded on the train's steps to sneak from one side of the river to the other. Étienne preferred to offer his services to English people. They paid well and exempted him from conversation, which he showed himself incapable of. *Yes, no, thank you*: that was the limit of his powers of expression. As for the rest, his gallantry and handsome little face went a long way. He had an air of honesty about him that inspired confidence. One regular tenderly referred to him as *my little frog.*

This is his first visit to the clubhouse this year. Every year, he comes now and again to proffer his services. He's a specialized caddie, meaning he helps beginners. There's always some idiot who, nearing forty, decides to become an athlete and shows up with a bagful of brand new golf clubs and a head stuffed with dreams of glory. Or a wife in her thirties who decides to cheat boredom while her husband is off killing himself at work or love. Étienne has seen enough good golfers in action that he can offer some useful tips, correct poor stances, recommend the right irons, and suggest the best way to get out of a bad lie.

Annie is at the counter, a nice girl with an imposing exterior who is sought after by no one and consoles herself as best she can. She welcomes the young man with her most winning smile.

"If it isn't my gorgeous Étienne!"

"Well, well! Annie herself! How are you?"

He places a kiss on her flabby cheek, which is instantly suffused with crimson. Her blue eyes stare at him intently, a little lost in the vastness of her face. He turns his head slightly to hide from her supplication. She inhales anyone who looks at her, sucks them in like a bottomless pit. Enough to give even an Indian vertigo, thinks Étienne, amused, picturing himself in the throes of grappling with this lump of fat flesh and sentiment. All the same, nice girls like Annie are rare; the object of her affections will be guaranteed perpetual adoration, not to mention constant devotion. For now, she languishes in her too-tight dresses: there really is no god of fat virgins.

"So," he asks. "Are you having a good year?"

"It's always a good year, Étienne. Golf is the only sport that never has a recession! The weather has to be really bad to keep the golfers away." Her mellifluous voice emits a flood of tedious remarks that seems like it will never end. When she pauses for breath, Étienne jumps in:

"Do you think I could make a little money this morning? Do old caddies like me still have a chance?"

"You know, caddies are kind of out of style right now. The players all have their pull carts, or else they rent electric carts. Though there are still a few eccentrics around who hanker after the good old days."

"What I'd like is someone who's just learning and needs some help."

"Hmm … The pro had better not catch you!"

"Don't worry, I'm in his good books."

"Okay, wait a second, I'll take a look at the bookings … Hmm, no, those are old regulars, and they really like their golf carts! They kick up a big fuss if I don't have any left! You really can't teach those guys a thing. Then … next, there's … yeah, maybe this guy, I've never seen his name before. He might be interested. Yeah, see that beanpole over there, coming this way? That's probably him."

Fifteen minutes later, Étienne is trying not to laugh at the beginner's struggles as he tries vainly to get his ball off the ground.

"Can I give you a tip?"

"What? Yes, yes, don't be shy. As you can see, I need all the advice I can get!"

The admission comes with a big smile, and Étienne almost recoils from it. He's so humble, it's almost shameless. Yet another masochist, Étienne says to himself, vaguely disgusted.

5

Father Lanthier is driving slowly toward the presbytery, his beautiful panama glued to his sinner's head. For a moment, he wonders whether he should instantly go and seek absolution from one of his colleagues, but he pictures himself in clothes defiled with the sweat of lust and longs only for icy water with which to scour away his vile sin. O Lord! How could he? At his age, with his experience, how could he have fallen for that witch's game? Yes, she's a witch, with the black cauldron of her sex, her great laughing lips with crooked teeth! He sees himself between the vampire's legs. Forgive me, Lord, forgive me for offending You! He prays, but the words carry the smell of flesh and hair; the abominably soft sensation of a woman's belly brushing against his — a belly that bathes daily in the river's silty water — tugs at his groin. O God, such softness! Never with Marthe, his housekeeper, has he known such complete delight. Marthe is simply a matter of hygiene, a monthly affair that has no further meaning and with which both God and the confessional are well acquainted. But Lucie! This is woman in all her horror! Woman as whore, as cunt. The hideous word returns to his lips ceaselessly, tainting them forever. Cunt!

He enters the presbytery like a hurricane and heads for his apartments, but Marthe, who had been on the lookout for him, intercepts him.

"Father, there's a man waiting for you. He's been here for almost an hour for a birth certificate."

"The office opens at one-thirty. You know that."

"Yes, but he's really in a hurry. He came all the way from Montreal."

"All right, I'll take care of it."

There's no time for solitary contemplation of his sin. His impure hands have touched the beautiful, sweet abomination; his hands, still glazed by pleasure, will perform the office of the priest, or rather the bureaucrat in charge of an administrative department that registers births and deaths, marriages and baptisms, all the acts that humans use to certify their presence on earth or their departure to the hereafter.

"You are … ?

"Vincent Lemire. Forgive me for coming at the wrong time, but I need a birth certificate urgently."

The man is in his thirties and fairly well dressed. He speaks correctly and with a certain ease. Could be in accounting, or insurance … As he fills out the certificate, Father Lanthier looks him over discreetly and wonders if he, too, is burdened with hidden sin, if his body bears the traces of shameful acts, if woman has enveloped him with her subtle contagion. Has he bathed in purifying water since the last time — probably last night — that he plunged his member into the soft abyss? More likely, the beaded secretions have dried on him. Beneath his brown suit, his air of decency, is he not one of the carnal's many minions, just like he is? A brother in slavery!

Father Lanthier signs with a slightly trembling hand and returns the document. He watches the hand reach toward him, wanting to take it and cover it in kisses, just to smell, breathe in the possibly guilty warmth, sniff the other's sin and at least find consolation in not being the only sinner. "The truth is, I'm going crazy," he says to himself, wanting to cry as the man takes out his money and hands him a large bill. He tries to give him some change, but the man stops him with a gesture — with that ambiguous, perhaps guilty hand.

"For the poor, Father. And many thanks for sparing me a two-hour wait."

He watches him leave, a fairly good-looking man, really, young; it is easy to picture him with a woman's breasts pressed against him, naked, all … God! God save me from my life!

Ten minutes later, although it is just before lunch and an odd time of day for it, Father Lanthier, armed with a horsehair bath glove, plunges himself into a tub full of cold water. He'd like to rip off his skin with it, but an image floats before him, no matter how hard he scrubs, an image with long, soft, undulating hair, over-large brown eyes, a sensuous mouth with large yellowy teeth, a demented laugh that pours over him like spittle, like a philtre, a sacrament, a heavenly blasphemy. And large breasts, moving, too white below the shoulders' bronze skin, breasts that descend like caresses, rain, smiling moons that have reinvented roundness, the fullness of his plunge, of sweetness.

Once again, he is overcome, he is hard to the breaking point in the icy water, which, far from appeasing him, exacerbates his tumescence to the point of pain. It is the devil, inside him, arousing him, possessing him, and damning him here and now in this tomb of icy metal. Stretched out on his back, legs apart, he imagines above him a vulva, red and black, descending toward him like the Pentecost, descending slowly toward his desire and misery, an enormous flower that will bury him in its smiling folds, envelop him in death. "Oh, God!" he whispers, and everything within him that responds to God's name fights the pounding of blood in his body, *hoc est enim* ..., the hiccups of the gorged beast, flesh desecrated, seed profaned.

6

The harsh midday light, just slightly tempered by a weak breeze, scorches everything, seeming even to penetrate the shadows gathered around the trees. Contrasts blur in the white air. The neighbours' radios and TVs can be heard blaring out various stations, intercut with brain-numbing commercials. Cooking odours and the sounds of dishes being washed emanate from several houses. At Lucie's, lunch is served on the veranda, whose enormous screened windows look out over the river. The room adjoins the kitchen, in which ground beef is sizzling.

Marie-Laure and Frédérique, the two oldest girls, are shuttling barefoot between the table and their mother, who's been making hamburgers and pouring ice-cold orangeade into glasses, non-stop. Tousled and sweating, the smell of her recent frolics noticeable from ten feet away, Lucie finds it hard to hide her satisfaction when she thinks of her recent victory over the priest. Now let the good Father try to lecture her! Let him try to side with the mayor against her! With one flash of desire, she has garnered his allegiance forever. She has nothing more to fear from him, from this essentially human personage with his podgy middle-class hide. He even managed to give her some pleasure, with his well-preserved virility and brand new desires — always exciting to find in a man that age. "That one must have spent more time on prayer than pleasure," she thinks, with a hint of pity. Now he's at her mercy. It's not that she wants to use his weakness to get undeserved favours from him: that's not her style. But at least she'll be able to count on being left alone to live in peace with her little ones.

"Children, do you want any more hamburgers?"

Her question doesn't penetrate the atmosphere enveloping the joyous table, which is replete with talk and laughter, the sounds of chewing and utensils. A peremptory noise ignites a burst of hilarity.

"You pig!" cries Marie-Laure, indignant, to an exultant Fernand.

"What's the matter? It's only natural! Here comes another one!"

The commotion begins anew, louder still. Before it can die out, Gervais brings it to a climax with a stentorian burp. Everybody is adding something to the general glee, some with their mouths and some otherwise. Only the two older girls want nothing to do with the gaiety, which Lucie listens to indulgently.

"Let them have their fun," she tells the girls. "It relaxes them, and they'll be quieter later."

"It's just too much, Mom, it's outrageous! I've never heard anything so rude!"

"Poor Marie-Laure! It's the nuns who are filling your head with those high ideas! If we had to listen to them, we'd never have any fun."

"Well, they're right in thinking that we Tourangeau kids are a badly brought up bunch!"

"What? What are you saying? Badly brought up? You'll find out one day, my girl, that having good manners is not about walking around with your thighs clenched or being as neat and shiny as a new pin. Being well brought up is about heart, generosity, and, as everybody knows, the Tourangeaus are generous to a fault."

"Generous, Mom! When we have to beg!"

"We don't beg, my dear! We take charity, which is different. But everything we get is owed to us, and don't ever forget that. The good doctor Tourangeau gave his all for this parish, up till his dying breath, and usually for nothing. Those who benefited can surely now honour us with their old clothes. What's more, I never asked those people for a thing. It was the priest who took it into his head to get us some help. He needed some poor people so he could perform his charitable works! Too bad for them. I'm not changing how I live or think, not one bit. Nobody's going to lecture me, understand? Do you understand, Marie-Laure? I just want you to realize that the nuns are hypocrites, and that my way of looking at things is the right way. Otherwise, you'll never be happy."

Marie-Laurie withdraws behind her pretty, stubborn features. She, like Gervais and Bernadette, has inherited her father's red hair and porcelain skin. Her distant Irish heritage sets her above this tribe, primarily made up of dark Mohawk complexions.

"Marie-Laure," inquires Fernand, "what do you do with your big farts? We never hear them!"

"I think she farts in her head," says Gervais.

"No," interrupts Vincent, a big Jules Verne fan, "she farts

faster than the speed of sound." There are great bursts of laughter at the idea.

"In *Around the Moon*," explains Vincent, "the characters wonder why they didn't hear the boom of the cannon that shot them into space. That's like us with Marie-Laure."

"Her big farts have put us into orbit around the moon," crows Gervais, as Fernand, dying of laughter, falls off his chair.

At the end of the table, Corinne and Stéphane listen to the noisy exchange, smiling and silent. As for the jibes aimed at Marie-Laure, only a glimmer of cruelty in their gaze attests to their participation in the overall glee.

"You're all ganging up on me. I'm leaving," Marie-Laure declares, taking off her apron.

"I'm with you," says Frédérique, getting ready to follow.

"Hey! You haven't eaten yet," Lucie interrupts. "Stay. Your brothers will apologize."

The two sisters leave the room, their heads held high, and the laughter subsides.

"Well, children, that's too bad for you. You, Gervais, are going to wash the dishes, and you, Fernand and Vincent, are going to dry."

Vehement protests ring out. Fernand clamours loudly that his health isn't good enough for that kind of thing, explaining objectively that, in a fit of anger, he might break all the dishes. Vincent alludes to the ones who never have to do any chores, eyeing his adopted siblings. Lucie lets the howls continue for a few minutes, then brings the swearing to an abrupt halt. An expression she knows how to put on — one of those inspired looks that have done much to establish her reputation for craziness — gets her silence and respect.

"She's going to hit!" Stéphane whispers to his sister.

He's extraordinarily tense, as if he were waiting for an old and familiar tale to repeat itself, a story in which, this time, he won't feature as the victim. Under the table, she takes his hand and squeezes it until it hurts.

"That one doesn't hit. She smothers."

7

God! he thinks. Great, holy God that I love and bless. The words tumble out confusedly. They're not a prayer, just a dogged, subconscious chant. Étienne sits on the strawberry-coloured vinyl seat, his face pummelled by the wind that enters the wide-open window. The car pitches over the flaws in the rails, shaking the passengers roughly. This is one of the few places where the train passes through true forest. Everywhere else, the landscape is studded with log houses from villages past, and, further along, by the bungalows and apartment buildings of the suburbs that border Montreal.

Shading his face with his hand to keep off the brisk wind as well as potential insects, Étienne watches an all-too-well-known landscape roll past as he ruminates over his familiar invocation. Vaguely, he ponders the hours he has just spent at the golf course, with that strange man who seemed more interested in talking than playing, and who begged him to call him by his first name. At first, he'd thought he was a homosexual, then had doubts. The man — Raymond — spoke of his son, who was about Étienne's age. He had dropped out of school and left home for the city, where he was living the most horrible of lives, as a drug addict and prostitute. The man talked of it with an odd smile that reflected despairing mortification and boundless astonishment at the turn his life had taken. In spite of his pain, he paraded his misfortune shamelessly, bombarding Étienne with confidences until he rebelled and told him, fairly rudely, that he didn't get paid to listen to people complain, which brought a still more sickly smile to the poor man's lips. Étienne finally escaped with an excellent tip and some syrupy praise.

The car — the only one open to passengers — is nearly full. Without thinking about it, Étienne is taking up more than his share of the narrow bench. The latest passengers to board don't dare claim the free seat, probably afraid of a hostile reaction from the scruffy young man with the broad shoulders. Étienne, however, comes out of his torpor when he catches sight of a ravishing girl standing a few feet away. This spectacle, or, rather, this apparition, instantly develops his social awareness, develops his understanding of life itself, for, in one instant, he is bowled over. Something, he doesn't know what, has pierced his heart and is stuck there, vibrating. The girl seems ordinary enough — she has two legs, two arms, some clothes, plus an adorable head — yet on seeing her, Étienne, unaccustomed to being lovestruck, feels a completely new sensation with unprecedented violence. Is it her smile, the quality of that smile that he glimpsed in a flash? Or the aroma that leapt on him like a playful breeze?

He instantly makes himself smaller, and his imploring gaze invites her to sit down next to him. She accepts the invitation easily, with a frank smile. Seated, her graceful knees peeping out below an elegant white skirt, she stares fixedly ahead. The train starts up again, with unaccustomed gentleness, it seems. Étienne is increasingly flustered and nervous. He feels distant from himself, as if he were as present to both his past and his future as to this moment. Dumbly, with an incredible clarity of sensation, he sees himself as a child, bending over an orangeade bottle that he fills with hot urine. Rough plants rub his thighs. He pushes this unclean memory away, and instead pictures great angels in lace, the Assumption of a lady all dressed in blue. This puts him on the trail of his actual feelings. He looks at her out of the corner of his eye, wanting to verify the miracle. Because this is truly a miracle: a woman such as he has never seen before, a combination of unimaginable graces, has materialized by his side. He must, he simply must speak to her to be sure that this moment really contains the opportunities he glimpses and that the day has truly taken a momentous turn. Arousal rises from his thighs, from his solar plexus, which is inundated with hot, rhythmic waves; he feels wonderfully strong. Strong and handsome. This exultation is so unexpected that he nearly utters Tarzan's grotesque, magnificent call, and he laughs, inwardly, full of joy. Like a breath, words cross his lips, effortlessly, predestined since time began — for this moment is nothing more or less than a gateway to eternity — and the words begin to etch simple arabesques around the other, around her.

She doesn't seem in the least bothered by having to talk to her neighbour. At first somewhat reserved, she replies with great kindness and, little by little, gives in to the pleasure of getting acquainted. In her deep green eyes, Étienne divines that she finds his face, his whole person, attractive, and even as he becomes aware of his own allure, he is yet astonished that he can exist in this way, instantly, so to speak, in a girl's appreciation, a girl who is all grace, who didn't even know him ten minutes ago, and who now, like a spray of water, a being composed of sun and silk, allows herself to be sensed and known by his side. She exists, he exists, together they are carried along by a single rectilinear steel fury toward the point where they will have to part, perhaps forever — but Étienne swears that it won't be so! Something too strong, too real is taking shape within this tremor of chance. What has been happening to him for the last few minutes is too astounding, too absolute, far too much like his heart's sweet words, his appeal to the great, good, holy God, for there to be nothing more.

Never, until now, has the young man ever felt so taken out of himself, so carried away from his familiar world and hurtled into a strange unknown, an unknown with a body and face that he feels he has always known, so fully do they meet his deepest yearning. How is it possible to discover, outside of himself, at such a point in time, something that so perfectly represents the most private rightness? Those eyes, so superbly green, moss and morning green, eyes opulent with dreams and goodness, new as the water between the lips of a stream — weren't they expressly intended for bringing daylight to the depths of a heart that has, until now, been devoted to groping blindly in the dark? Étienne feels solemn beside this gracious incarnation of a summer's morning. He is sombre, but a gay breeze rises within him, something he hasn't felt since his sunny childhood days. Oddly, his flesh is behaving perfectly, yet he feels like his gaiety could gust up, whirl out of control, that a sovereign rush of desire could rise from his loins and spread its magnificent terror through his entire body.

Yet here she is, young, fresh, beautiful, like a flower whose milky petals exhale light, petals veined with translucence, covered in minuscule parcels of mica, volumes of light and slenderness. Before her, raw desire could only become sprays of crystalline stars, cascading onto the body's deserted sands. Étienne would exist only as sky under this star's exhilarating influence; he would leave the desolate soil of his life far behind.

The most astounding thing is that the intoxication that has invaded him seems to be shared. He doesn't know how he knows this astonishing truth, but he is seized by an utter certainty, and it elates him. No longer does he exist only for himself. He now exists for her as well, just as she, with her grace and beauty, is now forever rooted in him.

At first, they talk mildly of trivialities, as if to remain at a safe distance from words that could instigate, alarm, hurry that which should be secret. He speaks carefully, though he has never learned the stratagems of seduction and has to trust his natural sensitivity. He talks, cautiously avoiding questions that are too direct. Suddenly, he hears himself, his voice like a masculine and joyous song in tune with hers, creating an astounding consonance of timbres, rising from their two bodies and uniting them.

Her name is Odile. She is going to Montreal for her weekly piano lesson, which she takes from an old lady who used to teach one of her aunts, and Étienne glimpses a world he has not dreamed of until now, a world of refinement in which Beauty holds prodigious rights.

When she asks him about school, about his plans, he is mortally anxious, and, to escape it, nearly resorts to fairy tales, but he recoils from the lie, for he has now placed himself in her light, in her, the font of bright and gentle truth. He looks at her, his eyes glowing with sincerity, and lets her know only that, for someone who cared, who would help him care, he could make his future matter.

The train enters the long tunnel under the mountain. Suddenly, he feels like the day has been turned upside down, that the miracle he's been experiencing for the last half-hour has been eclipsed without leaving a trace. But he gazes at her, and she turns to him with a look of tender companionship, and in it he sees acceptance of what he is, body and soul. He knows that, for her, he'd do something crazy, like go back to school, become somebody else, an auspicious man, swathed in light. Great, sweet God! What can have happened in those few instants to overturn his destiny, or rather, give it a proper perspective, make the person he was just that morning into a child he barely recognizes, from whom he is now separated by layers of solemn hope?

They roll together between the smooth tunnel walls, faintly lit by the car, a glittering block hurtling at a hundred kilometres an hour towards the rock's other side, where the city has laid out high towers of glass, steel, and granite on the chessboard of its streets. For ten minutes, under the mountain, they travel through a period of gestation as they await the return to open air. Their conversation has become more serious, they've made plans, holding themselves in this moment, mentally clinging to each other so they will never lose each other, making sure the miracle is anchored in their lives. Étienne had nothing particular to do in the city, so he will accompany Odile to her teacher's house (but won't show himself, to keep from arousing the old lady's affectionate curiosity) and wait for her in a small park nearby. After that, they'll be free for the rest of the afternoon. She had planned to go to the movies and she can easily make something up if her parents ask her any questions. She'll just draw on the vast store of movies she's already seen. But her parents trust her, and she probably won't need to call on her imagination.

Their plans are made and they gaze at each other, astonished at how much ground they've covered in so little time, little more than half an hour. Now they're like old friends; they have a wealth of history in common, created out of their most ancient yearnings, the secret hopes nurtured in the shelter of familial affections, ardent hours in which the flesh invents possessions that expand the soul and mould it into hope.

Étienne is still amazed that a girl so pretty, so sweet, whose pure existence seems so completely apparent in the elegance of her features, is not more sought after, is shown to him, available, as if the dice had always been cast in favour of this instant. How can he, poor, with no future set out for him, merit the prince's role? What glass slipper has he to offer her? But, from the few diplomatic words she has let fall, he understands that "until now" she hasn't been interested in boys, that all her time has been given over to her studies. And he basks in the intoxicating awareness that for him, and only for him, she has given leave to her austerity.

When they get off the train, he is carrying his new friend's thin black briefcase. Between their words and their gazes, the day's joy multiplies.

8

Under the oppressive light that assaults the houses and scorches the grass, summer's noises — a shrill humming of outboards
and lawn mowers, explosions of televised violence, the rare
screams of infuriated children or mothers — form the exact
reality of this torrid afternoon. For the last few weeks, the television at the Tourangeau house has been silent in response to
thuds intended to encourage it to yield a clearer picture. A solid
kick from Fernand administered its last rites. Since then, the
media barrage has given way to the drone of the kind of
unhealthy silence that hatches individual meditations. Lucie's
house is a like a mute hole amidst the well-kept houses nearby.
The lack of noise makes the cluttered yard and dilapidated
façade seem still more incongruous and ominous, as if irregular
ideas could develop there, out of reach of the common order
that is partly visual harmony and partly noise pollution.

After the meal, while the dishwashing operation was being
organized in an atmosphere of relative calm, Lucie lay down on
the big bed, nearly naked. Bernadette stretched out beside her
and fell asleep instantly. Lucie dozed, too, and now she daydreams, staring at the ceiling, her energy sapped by the heat she
loves, which is like a constant caress. Bernadette snores nearby,
free of underwear, with her short dress rolled up to her tummy.

When she awoke, Lucie admired her for a while, amazed, as always, by children's flesh, by the flesh of her child, full of grace and health. As a mother, she would like to have them all around her, from Étienne with his black gaze down to Bernadette, along with Corinne and Stéphane, the two children she gathered in. She wants them there, her whole tribe full of grace, truth, beauty, and for innocence to reign like heaven on earth, all together, unashamed, their frank nakedness a sacred offering. She would see them all, their lives unfolding: the males with their stirring virility, the little females with budding breasts and tufts like nests, luminous or dark. She'd count the belly-buttons, mete out compliments.

You, Vincent, are tough and serious, your eyes the colour of the ink they lick from the pages of books; you're as solid as a knot of roots. The woman on whom your kingly paw is placed will be very happy.

You, Étienne, my darling, you've got black eyes as well, but black as night, and sometimes stars shine gold lights in them because you're pure, great, noble, and your penis is a thick seedpod gorged with honey and wisdom.

Frédérique, my pretty dark mischief, with round breasts bruised by the purple of your large areolae, with eyes where dreams grow like tufts of rushes reflected in the water ... You got more than your fair share of your father's caresses. You were his adored papoose because of your rough hair and your vermilion-tinted cheeks. After playing with you, he would come to me, all wound up, and I'd have to calm those strong feelings.

Marie-Laure, Gervais ... you are red and white like matches. Your sharp, angular bodies remind me of Chonchon when I married him, and your green gazes are capable of anything, even love when the spirit takes you. But you, Marie-Laure, are playing the scornful virgin, and you, Gervais, what a shark you are behind that thin smile, when your whole being cries out mutely for pleasure. I know you, I love you as you are, warmed with your inner warmth, naked in your beauty, full of sex and sweetness, hands ready to melt the nugget of your dreams in the fire of this life, which has no chance of being beautiful and just unless it is embraced with open arms, bedded and violated under your flat stomachs.

Then she pictures them one by one, her boys and her girls, stretched out next to her and each in their way impregnating her with their quivering youth, filling her with caresses and ecstasy, making her throb with the enormous love from which they issued, cells long incubated and multiplied become hands and buttocks, saliva and cries, great vehement bodies creating in her rain and sun, one by one, with the fullness of their glowing flesh.

Then she pushes the images away. She's not really ashamed, but she knows that these are futile dreams, and affection and desire can't be blended. She will not lie down with her family, her boys, her girls, her beloved flesh. Her skin will not receive their babbling love. Maybe God exists and wants ardour to leave its native hearth behind, set other heavens ablaze. And if God does not exist, there remains that which causes him to be imagined, with his steel-armoured laws. Let the sword sunder, let it separate mother and child, and thus give love the chance to be holy.

The idea sends a ripple of laughter through her. Holiness! She pictures the priest, a worthy man if there ever was one, with his starched charities and rituals. Men like him are the easiest to manipulate. Their definition of life is so false, their idea of women so unhealthy that the slightest direct assault, the slightest whiff of truth, incapacitates them completely. I'm his skid row orchid, she thinks. For him, I'm a blossom in the mud, his twinkling passion star. I'll show him the difference between the hosts of heaven and the worms of this earth, teach him about the things of this world. She calls up his naked face, stripped of the wire-rimmed glasses that give him a civilized air, sees the pale blue eyes unable to focus, appalled by the sin that is so sweet and good that it undoes his courage. His close-ly shaven cheeks are riddled with tiny cropped hairs, white in some places and black in others. His cheeks are a black and white field, the light reflecting off its waxy surface. Though his hairline has receded, his forehead doesn't have the obscene look so common to the ridiculous contours of bald heads.

Plus, this man smells of good soap. It's nice to take a clean lover to bed, for a change. Her usual partners are more unbri-dled, and not always very appetizing, either, with their barbar-ic looks. A priest among the barbarians, that's like having an Our Father among all those Hail Marys, Lucie tells herself. It nourishes sex, gives it dignity! She smiles, a little frightened by the idea of blasphemy, even more afraid of damning a man of God forever. But no, if God exists, he'll save his servant and he'll save me, too, because I'm a good mother hen with my chicks around me, and all I ask from life is a little happiness and pleasure. Joy, enjoyment — they're almost the same word, really. That's what makes life bearable while you wait for what's to come. Once you're dead, there's no more pleasure.

Bernadette moans softly in her sleep, and a smile lights her face. She's so beautiful, so radiant that Lucie is moved to tears. She bends over the chubby angel, born from her flesh, contemplates her lovingly, blows very lightly on her white genitals, stops herself from kissing them, licking, eating them like a tender Eucharist. Bernadette moves, half-wakened by the flow of air between her thighs, and falls back into the flush of dreams, where all is promise.

"Mom! Mom! Come quick! Corinne is drowning!"

Fernand is standing at the door, shouting. Jerked out of her drowsiness, Lucie realizes what's going on instantly and races outside, nearly naked in her bra and ragged panties. The children's shouts have alerted two neighbours, who are rushing over, but Lucie, with a moan like a wounded animal, has beaten them to the water and is swimming to where she saw the still body floating. It's right by the big whirlpool and could be carried into the rapids. Her expert strokes cut rapidly through the water, but her panic adds a certain feverishness. When she gets to the place, she searches around desperately, then dives.

For two long minutes, the water remains closed over its secret like a seal, revealing nothing of what destiny holds in store. The neighbours, meanwhile, have gone to get their boat and are clumsily making their way to the scene. They catch sight of a thin figure surfacing to the right, and Lucie emerges from the water several feet away, out of breath. They shout directions and point at the floating thing. Finally, she understands and makes her way to the body, reaching it just as it's about to go under once more. The boat gets there seconds later, and they hoist the little girl aboard, followed by an exhausted Lucie. They hurry back to shore and Lucie, instantly revived, races with the inert form to the edge of the lawn and starts to administer the necessary treatment. She rolls the child onto her stomach and forces the water out of her, pressing on her shoulder blades to make her breathe. Grim and determined, speaking only to forbid the neighbours to call the police, she kneads the body, convinced that her hands, formed for strangling and giving life, can rekindle the tiny spark. Fernand, Vincent, and Stéphane are gathered around her, and Stéphane contemplates his sister with a kind of sacred terror. The two big girls, Marie-Laure and Frédérique, are trying to calm Bernadette, who is shaking with sobs. They are torn between the feeling that Corinne has left them forever, that her soul has stayed behind at the whirlpool's depths, separated forever from the water-logged body that is paler than soap, and the conviction that, with her great hard arms pushing breath into the child, Lucie, their mother, can cheat death and force her to resume the chore of living.

Finally, her maternal tenacity triumphs. Ten interminable minutes later, there's a little moan, and tears start to stream from the beneath the closed eyelids. An explosion of joy follows, and Lucie, her warm voice rich in harmonies, cries out beneath the stately trees, "Thank you, God! I knew you wouldn't let the child die!"

But Stéphane, his cheek pressed against his sister's, hears her whisper: "Damn her! I wanted to drown ... I'd be so happy if I was drowned ..."

With the danger past, the neighbours want to get away, more and more embarrassed by Lucie's indecent appearance. Still unconscious of her near nudity and wanting to show that everything's back to normal, Lucie confides, "I hope this won't make her afraid of the water!"

9

After Odile's piano lesson, which took place in a narrow, venerable house on Sherbrooke Street, just west of Atwater, with her glowing presence beside him, focused on him, Étienne is happy once more. How he has changed! He feels so different from the futureless young man he was this morning, entangled in resentments and small disappointments, sitting on his cheap mattress in that bleak room. His heart sinks at the thought of home, and he'd like to never go back there. The thought of his noisy brothers, his sisters, his slovenly mother, the base familiarity that holds them under a single roof, sampling shameful pleasures, alienates him from what his life has been and sparks a yearning for a new existence, completely cut off from his past, built from the love that flows through his whole being. Beside him, with her long iridescent hair, her gaze miraculously friendly and pure, her adorable nose, her lightly arched mouth, the chin that sticks out a little, giving her whole face character, and, most of all, her air of kindness, intelligently gentle, her unaffected nobility, *she* is something he had never hoped to meet, that he had only glimpsed from time to time in TV movies. She is youth and beauty, tenderness and simplicity that have grown together, blended, away from mutilating torments and social evils. Refinement! She has been refined from birth, Étienne tells himself. She has grown up with beauty around her, unlike his own sisters, especially Marie-Laure, who wants so much to conform to the narrow mould set out by the nuns who teach her, while her frustrated nature, like her impertinent red-headed complexion, constantly pierces through beneath her air of acquired distinction.

"Where are we going now?" asks Étienne, when they have taken a few random steps.

"Let's go to the mountain!"

Hand in hand, they start to walk toward Côte-des-Neiges Road, which connects with one of the forest's main paths. The intense heat is slightly mitigated by the breeze on the mountain's slope, and they're careful to stay in the shade cast by the houses and tall trees. As they climb higher, more and more of the immense sun-bathed landscape stretches behind them, a mosaic of roofs that, in the distance, blends with greenery, the river's calm lines stretching through a haze of light that blurs the horizon a little but lets the ghostly profile of the closest Monteregian hills show through.

"Look! You can see Mont-Saint-Bruno and Mont-Saint-Hilaire," says Odile, pointing. "Have you ever been there?"

"No … I'm a bit familiar with the countryside around my house, up to Oka, and I know Montreal pretty well, but I've never travelled. You know …"

He looks at her, embarrassed. She smiles so warmly at him that he finds the right words to confide in her. "My parents aren't very well off. And, well, they don't live together anymore. Like they say, I'm from an underprivileged background."

There is, in the Big Bang of first love, a velocity of feeling that allows the myriad facets of personal and family life to be embraced, no matter how delicate, no matter how private they usually are. An energetic grace works to choose the words, shines light on the shadows, provides the eloquence that makes everything understood with little said, and hastens toward the conclusion, a kiss. The goal of the first strides in love is a total baring of the soul, which operation clears the way for the body's wondrous desire and luminous raptures.

It is toward this unveiling of souls that Étienne and Odile walk with slow steps in the gleaming shade below tall trees in which squirrels and birds mount their furtive ambushes. Étienne mentions his large family, his commitment to them, but also his frustration, his yearning to escape, to get away from the idleness and petty prospects imposed on him by his mother. Odile talks about the punctilious affection she gets from her father, who still thinks of her as a little girl, and about her mother's effaced personality — she's devoted her life to serving her husband and educating her children. Her mother decidedly prefers Simon, the eldest, who is studying in the States and wants to be a neurosurgeon. And her dad — did she mention it already? — is a lawyer for a big drug company.

"So, you see," she concludes, "money doesn't mean anything. To live with ... the man I love, I'd leave everything behind. True wealth lies in the heart."

Étienne smiles sadly. "Things aren't that simple ..."

For a minute, they are both silent, then he speaks again, overcome with joy. "It's so beautiful today! The light through the trees is so moving, with the birds singing, the amazing peace! The city feels so far away! Like we're far from everything, and there's only us, just our arms, our hands ... When you smile like that, it feels like heaven on earth. You're an angel, you know, but much better than an angel."

"I hope so!" she says. "Angels must be annoying creatures. They surely can't savour a moment like this. Look at those trees, so straight, so heavy — yet they don't seem solid at all, they seem like illusions. Weighty illusions ... Good Lord, I must be delirious! Angels aren't made of matter, either, but they don't weigh anything, they're not hot or cold, and their hands have no volume, no ..."

She stops and, very serious, takes Étienne's hand in hers, then carries his broad, square palm to her lips. Suddenly he is overcome, and the outline of his erect penis is so clear against the denim of his jeans that Odile, flustered, puts an end to her caress.

"We mustn't ... we mustn't rush anything."

Deeply moved, Étienne still finds the strength to laugh. "No ... No, my angel!"

She sighs.

10

This is the time when Lucie, arrayed in her flowered bathing suit, usually walks down to the river and, after a conspicuous sign of the cross, enters the living water that is like a cloth, smoothed out by invisible hands just for her. But today she won't swim with long, slow strokes, nor will she rest, upright, above the drop-off, musing on the remnants of domesticity entrusted to its depths forever, old fridges and stoves, mattresses and box springs no longer in use. Perhaps this evening, once the house and her soul have calmed down, she will do what she loves best, naked under the stars' complicitous glimmer. But nothing is as good as her five o'clock swim, when the wind has dropped and the water is a great soft mirror that she splits, like an inverted sky, amidst the dance of water beetles. This ritual is so important to Lucie that she almost succumbs to its call, but a glance at the thin form huddled in the big bed banishes temptation. How pale she is! How awfully thin! The skin on her face is too fine and the delicate bones show through it. She would be beautiful but for the utter lack of joy that hollows her cheeks, shapes her features into an image of endless darkness. What memories stored in that head keep her from smiling? Corinne has never confided in her new mother about the abuses she suffered when she was younger. Lucie has heard rumours of long hours spent cruelly tied to a bed frame, but she suspects other kinds of violence, too, not just physical. The household lived off welfare, and the mother paid for drugs through prostitution.

With this ruin of childhood before her, Lucie's heart aches as if these things had happened to her, as if the blind justice of the world had come down on her with its iron fist. Anything that affects young children touches home and makes her capable of the greatest sacrifices. If any vocation could be said to illuminate her muddled life and dictate the right decisions to her, it is motherhood. She doesn't understand how a woman could be so immoral as to abandon her children. Nor can she understand — this is the theme that sometimes turns her into a fierce militant who travels to Montreal, leaving the older children in charge of the younger ones — how incautious or abused girls could have the seed of a human destiny extracted from them like an appendix or a bad tooth. Where is humanity heading, Lord, when the very foundations of society, of the family, are put into question, and kindness no longer characterizes how we deal with each other? It doesn't matter how many solid, practical arguments are put forward by the middle class, Lucie is still for life. She'd like to see abortionists thrown in jail along with all the other murderers. What an abomination, legalizing the worst crime there is — cutting a life off before it can even begin to bloom, taking away its only chance to develop and thrive, crushing the flower in its perfect bud!

Before the pale child, who is barely breathing, her eyes obstinately sealed over a sadness that has permanently taken root, Lucie asks heaven for guidance to help her drive the misery out and plant joy and confidence where the wounded beast now writhes in pain.

She hears a small noise at the bedroom door and notices Stéphane, discreet as always, watching her indecisively, as if afraid to make the slightest move.

"Come in, Stéphane. Come closer," encourages Lucie in a low voice. "Come see your little sister. She looks like an angel!"

Timidly, he stands next to Lucie, who, with her stature and opulent flesh, looks like a giant beside him. He leans over Corinne's face and, moved, Lucie puts her hands on the two frail shoulders and pulls him to her. He yields a little, but seems ready to run the instant she relaxes her grasp. After a few minutes, she notices that, without a sound, without a sob, he has begun to cry, and tears are falling from his open eyes. The tears' source distills such despairing pain that it is lost, drop by drop, in a desert of silence. What kind of appeal to God could abolish so much suffering and bring sunshine into young souls who have never seen it dawn?

A powerful and grotesque sound rends the dimness. It comes from the street, and Lucie is outraged that this horn could disturb the little girl's sleep. Leaving Stéphane to watch over Corinne, Lucie races outdoors. An excited Tourangeau tribe has converged on a car that is parked above the property and honking without respite.

"Stop! Stop!" begs Lucie. "You'll wake the sick child!"

Her voice can't be heard over the racket, but Fernand and Vincent have seen her and hang onto her, retailing the miracle. She rebuffs their gay outbursts so categorically that she manages to get their attention, and the wild honking strangles on a final blare.

"Would you stop this racket! Your little sister Corinne is trying to sleep. And you, Gervais, what do you think you're doing driving that car?"

"Corinne's sick?" inquires Gervais.

"Yes, she nearly drowned. We managed to save her, but just barely. Do you really think this is a good time for your non-sense? What are you doing in that old car?"

"Mom, this is Denis's car. He lent it to me — right, Denis?"

The fat boy seated on Gervais's right nods his head silently.

"Denis," continues Gervais, "works at Carrier's garage. He bought this antique for a hundred dollars and fixed it all up. It's a real collector's item now! And it runs like it's almost new. It's a Durand from the forties. He got it from an old guy who had it in his garage."

Baffled, Lucie examines the inside of the car, squalid with age and dust.

"But you don't have a driver's licence."

"No, but Denis is right beside me, and he's got his papers — right, Denis?"

Denis nods, staring at Lucie with empty eyes.

"What if you have an accident? What if the police stop you?"

"Come on, Mom! That's not going to happen. First of all, I'm a great driver. And, if anything does happen, like I told you, Denis is here. We just have to change places. So don't get all worried for nothing."

Lucie hesitates for a few minutes and then allows him to win her over. Gervais looks so happy, so proud, as if he were driving his own first car. She can't prevent a smile and says, at last, "Okay then. All right, but you've got to promise you won't do anything stupid."

"Hurray!" the children yell, anticipating hours of thrilling outings.

"Not so loud! Corinne is sleeping! And, Gervais, I forbid you to let any of your brothers and sisters ride in this old clunker."

The protests are so lively that poor Lucie is forced to beat a retreat. "Okay, okay, but if something happens, don't come running to me!"

Cheers ring out, completely destroying Corinne's last hope of sleep.

11

When he's fed up with working on his little "dolls" — Chimeras by Chonchon! What a life! — and looking out for customers — a condescending tourist or *petit bourgeois* after the perfect status symbol for his child, one that'll make friends and neighbours writhe with envy — Chonchon himself, in person, opens his desk drawer and pulls out the green bottle with the red and white label. Just the sight of it makes his entrails quiver with pleasure, or, specifically, the area around his navel, which must be fairly parched, for keeping it hydrated seems like a never-ending job. He brings the bottle to his lips, and the delicious geneva gin slips down his throat, blazes, braces, clearing his pipes and producing a sensation at the top of his nose that feels like a tiny punch, just the thing for making him think clearly. Ah! The merciful mouthful that scrubs your carcass out on the inside and subdues it, makes it smooth and youthful, ripe for a red-nailed caress, nails that are too red, the colour of fresh blood, the vampish nails of my vampire — vampire by Chonchon! The gin, a thin stream of thunder, moves through his body like water through a baby doll. You give them the bottle, and there it is, right away, I drink you, you drench me, instantly I'm flooded from head to toe with your liquid caress, and my fabulous reproductive organ awaits the caress of crimson nails, my Vanessa, my delicious slut full of little screams of ecstasy, where are you, my love? Oh, that's right, you're only coming home at seven, I forgot about your taping session, and I hope you're having fun with your burly guys. One day, I'll kill them all, but I'm in no rush — once their big dicks have made you come, you come to me, all horny, enchanting me with your bewitching caresses, and it's almost like I'm watching you on video, smiling, working on my thin chest, your nails furrowing it like fresh, burning wounds.

At the thought of Vanessa, of the happy ravishers' hands on her creamy flesh, he gets a slight hard-on and takes another swig of gin. Hah! It cures everything, even shame. As for the rest, Chonchon isn't given to strong feeling. He came to terms with certain frailties a long time ago — his weakness, indolence, an irrefutable cowardice when faced with suffering, a shunning of responsibility, his absence. Absence, especially. Chonchon is never there for anyone. Knock on the glass of his sullen shopfront and the blinds close instantly, the eyes become veiled, an air of subtle stupidity creeps over his face, from the balding forehead, wrinkled and obscene, to the indeterminate chin. Where is the man who created all these friendly fantasies, the ones that charmed childhoods with their priceless expressions, multi-eyed pig-penguins, cassowary-firemen, little prima donnas with three behinds? He has rendered even atrocities loveable, disarming horror, consecrating folly, drawing on all the hiccups in the system. Customers are invariably seduced by an elusive question that these disjointed toys pose with their sordid appearance, a question immediately withdrawn in the calm certainty that it has no answer, that childhood is a marvellous rite of passage that leads directly to total absolution.

Chonchon loves children and has nothing but contempt for parents, particularly parents who demand the most expensive chimera, the one that is the most decidedly "Chonchon." They depart with fragments of his dream like Christians with a piece of the true cross. But his dream is inexhaustible, for money, it goes without saying, is a good fertilizer, just like gin. Inspiration takes shape between his hands each morning, not too different, all in all, from what Vanessa's beautiful body stimulates in her film-making friends.

A man has to live, after all, sell a bit of fantasy for as much money as possible, though there's never enough money to subdue true repugnance.

It's nearly seven. Chonchon doesn't have the heart to start a new piece, so he contents himself with waiting for customers, who are unlikely to appear at this point. Yet, here's a woman, fiftyish, probably just wanting to sniff things out. She'll ask a lot of questions and recoil at the prices.

"Are you Mr. Chonchon?"

"At your service, madam."

"Well, you're a polite one! That's not your real name, is it? Chonchon?"

"In fact, to my knowledge, there has never been a saint with that name. It's a sobriquet."

"A so … a so… What's your real name?

"Tell me, dear lady, do you work for the RCMP? Or for Revenue Canada?"

"Don't get mad, I was just curious. So, you're the one who makes those little monsters?

"As you put it," says the craftsman. He can feel the gin surging back up his throat in small, acid explosions.

"Cute! Hey, this little doll here looks just like my husband."

"My condolences."

"Pardon?"

"Nothing ... Are you looking for a gift?"

"No, no. I wasn't planning to buy anything, if that's what you're asking. As I was walking by, I saw the sign saying Please Come In, so in I came, that's all."

"Well, then, madam, there's nothing to keep you from going out, even if you haven't received a written invitation."

"Well! You're not quite as polite as before, are you? I thought you looked like a bit of a hypocrite, too."

"And what about you, madam?"

"Who, me?"

"Yes. I'd rather look like this than like a dirty old sponge that's been soaking in a tub full of shit and vomit."

"What?"

"I've got no time to waste on a freak like you."

Staggering a little, the fat woman dashes out, muttering insults: "He's crazy, that one! What an idiot! Treating customers like that. If he thinks I'm going to encourage him, he'd better think again. I've never seen anything like it!"

On her way out, she bumps into a young couple, who step aside to let her pass. Chonchon turns a stern gaze on the newcomers, and his eyes widen in surprise.

"Étienne! I'll be damned, this is an unexpected pleasure."

"Hi, dad. Uh … dad, I'd like you to meet Odile, my girlfriend."

"Well, what a surprise! Since when have you started going out with girls? And a pretty one, too!"

Odile holds out her hand, but Chonchon kisses her on both cheeks, full of affability. "When I see pretty young things like you, I just have to kiss them!"

The young people both laugh, and Étienne explains, "We were in the neighbourhood, and Odile wanted to see your workshop."

"Yes," she adds. "One of the best presents I ever got when I was little was one of your famous chimeras, Mr. Tourangeau, a little old woman with several noses, with a top half like a two-tiered wood stove, and a bottom like a vacuum cleaner with several tentacles coming out of it. It's wonderful how all the parts are so different, but they go together so well you'd think such a creature really existed."

"Now, that makes me happy," says Chonchon, puffing up. "That really makes me happy. I love meeting people who've lived with my monsters, given them homes, made friends with them …"

"They're not monsters," protests Odile. "On the contrary!"

"What a sweetheart your girlfriend is, Étienne! Have you known each other long?"

"Since this morning. We met on the train."

"Well, you seem to be made for one another."

A big smile lights up Étienne's face. Though he'd dreaded this visit, he's realizing he had nothing to worry about. He can breathe easy in this workshop, which now holds new interest for him. When he came here as a child, he was entertained by the baroque faces, the transcendent farces that his serious, almost sullen father created while gulping firewater out of that green bottle. Étienne had tasted the gin once and thought he was going to die of it. Mainly though, when he came to visit, he just waited around, bored, for his mother to come for him. He and she would leave, laden with packages from the big department stores. Before Grandma Lintvelt went into the home, excursions into the city were possible because she took care of the little ones. Lucie hasn't been shopping for a long time. The successive pregnancies have now wrapped Lucie permanently in poverty, which she wears with an air of nonchalance. She's proud of how healthy she looks and pays little heed to the rags on her back, rags whose stunning sloppiness sometimes make her look like one of Chonchon's chimeras.

"They're incredible, Mr. Tourangeau!" exclaims Odile, delighted with each of the figures. "I don't know how you manage to do all this, just with plush. And they're all so different. It's like you've combined all three kingdoms: animal, vegetable, mineral …"

"Plush, little lady, is my specialty. For one thing, I want to make objects that children can touch without getting hurt. For another, even the worst horrors become friendly when they're made from plush. If it's easy on the hand, it's easy on the heart."

"I know where dad gets his ideas," says Étienne, laughing. "In here!" He grabs the bottle, opens it, and takes a sip.

"Étienne, you little rat! Just look at that! You've got no respect for your old dad! Do you want to make her think I'm a drunk?"

"No, an alcoholic."

"Hey, Vanessa, do you hear that?"

Her name causes a stir, and they turn toward the newcomer. Her excessive blondness and thick makeup mark her as a pleasure professional at first glance. Étienne has heard his mother refer to her in unflattering terms, and struggles to be polite.

"Good afternoon, ma'am."

"Skip the formalities," says Chonchon, "it's just Vanessa. Vanessa, I'd like to introduce my son, Étienne, and his pretty little girlfriend, Odile."

Vanessa greets them with a frightened smile and takes refuge beside Chonchon.

"So, did you have fun?"

"Yes," she says, embarrassed.

"Vanessa is an actress," he explains. "She makes videos. Right?"

"Yes."

The vanilla perfume diffused by Vanessa's indiscreet flesh now permeates the room. Behind her showy looks, the woman seems rather shy and very kind. Her vulgar flashiness is poles apart from Odile's fresh beauty, however, and the latter can't quite recover her demeanour. The atmosphere is somewhat uncomfortable, and Étienne breaks the silence, announcing, "Odile and I are going to get going. We haven't eaten yet."

Chonchon and Vanessa ask them to stay for supper, they'll order out, but Étienne refuses, and they don't insist. Chonchon slips a twenty-dollar bill into his son's fist, who looks quite upset at first, but finally accepts. It's a relief to be out on the street once more, but he's worried about how Odile is reacting. Sensing his embarrassment, she gives him a big, reassuring smile.

"She's very nice," she says.

"Yeah. Well, she's the perfect kind of girl for my father, anyway."

"He's very nice, too."

"He's spineless. And what's more, he's unbelievably selfish. The only thing he cares about is his bottle," he says, pretending to take a swig.

He instantly scolds himself for being so harsh and crude, however. What's she going to think of me? You shouldn't judge your own father. Frustrated, he takes a deep breath and stops, looks into Odile's eyes, matches his smile to hers as the sweet vibrations of desire rise within him, already laden with remembrance.

That afternoon, on the mountain, after they'd exchanged pasts in the form of bittersweet stories that nonetheless spared their parents, they explored deserted areas and ventured their first caresses, astounded to be coming to this shared fervour so quickly, without having rushed anything. Although, as well-behaved children, they are inexperienced, being eighteen gave their emotions some resolve and steered them towards the conjunction of gestures, the gentle contact between the storms within their bodies. They didn't dare embark on more intimate caresses, the kind that would lead to something irreversible, yet their hands slid to the edges of the forbidden, then returned to their clear countenances. They possessed each other only with looks and lips and, embraced, they drank of each other at length.

Then Odile remembered her train, and they started down
the mountain. On the way, however, she announced, "Darn it,
I'll go home later. I'm not a child anymore. But I should let my
parents know, so they don't get worried." She stopped at a
phone booth, and Étienne watched as she explained, not without difficulty, then hung up the phone somewhat abruptly.
"They're not used to it," she said, laughing. Then they decided what to do with the next few hours. "Didn't you tell me that
your father's workshop was in Old Montreal?" Étienne was not
very enthusiastic but, remembering Odile's surprise and delight
when he'd mentioned the famous craftsman, he agreed, though
warning her, "You know, my father's a real bohemian … and a
bit inclined to drinking." They decided to drop by anyway; if
there was a problem, they'd slip away.

The visit turned out well, all in all. Odile contemplated
the lair where the adorable chimeras are made, and their creator, overlaid with Étienne's fine filigree, appeared fairly pleasant. Artists have their eccentricities, after all. And, well, the
marvellous chaos that characterizes the plush toys "by
Chonchon" must, of course, have its source in the life of their
creator. That's how she explains it to her partly Mohawk
Adonis, who, with his slender frame and the dark beauty of his
features, is so different from his father's bald, Irish, and somewhat shopworn identity.

12

"Great holy great holy great holy God," chants Étienne to himself. He's walking on the ties between the rails, which are lit now and then by street lamps. Most of the time he can barely see, but a sort of instinct guides him and keeps him from turning an ankle. He is so filled with joy that he's nearly dancing and almost bursting with a supreme agitation, compounded by the suppressed impulses that have accumulated in his body over the course of the day. He tries to contain himself, then is forced to yield to his pressing excitement. He stops, and, gently, making each gesture pure by thinking of the holy union that will one day join him to Odile, flesh to flesh, he caresses himself to the point of ecstasy, long delayed. As he comes, he moans God's name, blended with hers, the name of the divine companion, the girl with the adorable face from whom he has just parted, a few steps away from her house, whom he embraced, running his hands over her shoulders, down her back, then slipping a hand towards her breasts, which felt naked under her blouse, the breasts whose hard tips he brushed through the thin cloth. And, with her palm, she touched his distended jeans, then tore herself away. "Goodbye, my prince," she said, "until tomorrow."

They are to meet on the golf course, the golf course where Étienne set out on his adventure at the beginning of the staggering day that is now coming to a close. That broad green space is only two or three kilometres from where she lives. The thought of such a meeting place occurred to them by accident, and Étienne had exclaimed, "You play golf?" The thought that he might have come across her before they'd met astounded him. "Quite badly, actually. I've got no aptitude for it. It was my parents who wanted me to sign up. They don't think I get enough exercise. But it seems to me that they're thinking about my future; and the golf course seems like a good place to meet people ..." The remembered words tumble in Étienne's head as he finishes appeasing himself.

Then he starts forward again. A few minutes later, he's at the edge of the golf course and decides to cross it. He climbs the chain-link fence, as he did so often as a child, and finds himself under the tall pines that border the property. There's something frightening about the impenetrable shadows, but the intense aroma of resin reassures and relaxes him. Not a star in the sky. Muffled rumbles presage a storm, swollen with the day's mugginess. Even if he runs, it will take Étienne at least ten minutes to reach the bridge. He moves away from the row of pines and sets off across the green, where he can move more easily. A few moments later, he feels the first drops, and then the rain comes down heavily. He veers back under the trees, which stand out clearly against the blazing sky. The interval between lightning and thunder is still considerable. To save time, he steps back into the rain, which has quickly soaked him through. A kind of exhilaration takes over, prompting him to push his body to its limits. His youth exults in this expense of gestures in the rain, in the face of the storm that is whipping out bolts of lightning and could stop him cold, crucify his mortal insignificance. But he loves, he is a god, and the storm respects those whose bodies and souls bear the sacred flame. In the lashing, caressing rain, he purses his lips, kissing the night's warm-water hand, embracing the weight of water and shadow that reveals its secret to him. It is as if he were naked, his hair dripping down his neck, his clothes pressing their sodden affections on him. In the distance, he hears the furious barking of the Great Dane, fortunately penned in his enclosure behind the clubhouse.

Suddenly, lightning, followed instantly by a deafening noise, envelops him in its flash of daylight and stops him. This time, he's afraid. Should he retreat once more under the shelter of the pines? It's probably wiser to lie on the ground, not too close to the trees, but not too far, either, where the treetops will draw the lightning to them. His heart racing, head buried in folded arms, back pounded by the heavy rain that forms puddles around him, he waits for the next lightning strike, completely powerless against the raging storm, and a kind of admiration for the storm's spectacular intensity slowly enters him. The sky seems to be resolving itself into a barrage of fire and tears against the earth, the vastness filled by a single event in which nothing and no one has any separate existence. It is like the great deluge, and suddenly Étienne can no longer resist the spectacle. He rolls onto his back, opens his eyes wide, drinks in the dazzle and din, focuses on God amidst the onslaught of smoke and water, and suddenly starts to sing a

bizarre chant that rises from his depths, a song like the ances-
tral songs that Lucie sang without understanding them, but
herself comprehended by these words without form, these
heartfelt rhythms. Undoubtedly, he celebrates the girl more
beautiful than a star, than lightning, than the stream's throaty
laugh, the girl whose body is so near his soul that a single dawn
blesses them. Then, immunized against his fear, he sets out
once more through a night that is at times suspended for a few
trembling moments by hallucinatory days that unveil distant
spaces with apocalyptic light. Were lightning to strike at his
feet, he would push it from his path without a word. Were it to
descend upon him, he would clasp it to him and break its black
spine. Étienne is a force of self against the world. A self full of
joy and the radiance of dawn. Faced with him, night can do
nothing but try to hold its own.

He reaches the fence, and, climbing it once more, finds
himself on the railroad tracks, close to the bridge. With no
lighting, the tracks bury themselves in darkness, made more
impenetrable still by the bad weather. The gorge opens up
between the wooden ties, which glisten with black water. Étienne hesitates, then starts onto the tracks. At that very
moment, he hears the locomotive's bell. The train, now in the
station, will be starting back toward Montreal, and will pull up
after the bridge. Étienne quickly retraces his steps and hides,
out of the conductor's sight. He takes refuge under the
guardrail, and, for a moment, considers swimming across, but
what would he do with his clothes? With the current and
whirlpools, the slightest weight is a hindrance. And it's too big
a risk. Even during the summer, the water's power could sweep

him along and dash him on the rocks.

A few minutes later, after the train has passed and the rail's vibrations have abated, he tries his luck again. This time, his feet are bare so he can feel the wood properly and keep from slipping. He quickly gains confidence. At the middle of the bridge, he remembers the morning's gesture with a smile, the prolonged micturition of an urchin who is happy to relieve himself in broad daylight, connect with the vast water and with nature, liberate himself, between these shores, from the ill humours amassed in the labyrinthine house. He pictures Odile catching him in this posture and suddenly feels above such things, more mature in comparison with his previous life, which came to an end between eleven o'clock and noon today, when the sweetest of thunderbolts sat down by his side.

The storm has moved on, carrying away its cannons and torrents. A calm rain has taken its place, and the air is rapidly cooling off. In his wet clothes, Étienne feels chilly. He's now coming to the end of the bridge, happy that he hasn't picked up a splinter, and starts to hurry toward the big blue house.

It's still raining when Étienne gets home, and the thought of stripping off his wet clothes and slipping under dry sheets, warmed by Gervais, makes him happy. But near the entryway, under the small overhang, a shape draws his attention. At first, he barely recognizes it.

"Is that you, Mom?"

There is no answer, which comes as an intense surprise. He draws closer and discovers a Lucie so deprived of her usual exuberance, so sunk in some dismal meditation, that he is suffused with embarrassment.

"Has something happened?"

She utters an almost inaudible groan, impossible to interpret. He slips his arm around her, puts his hand on her shoulder, something he has never done before but that he can now do, now that he's a man and he loves a woman and the body has become feeling's natural channel. She shivers under the caress.

"You're wet. You're soaked. Go get changed, quickly, or you'll catch your death."

"I'll be right back."

He climbs the stairs, tripping on the scattered clothing, and enters the boys' room, which is faintly illuminated by a night light. He notices that Gervais isn't there. Vincent and Fernand are sleeping heavily.

Free of his sodden clothes, Étienne casts his eyes around and sees nothing to wear but an old, beltless bathrobe. He puts it on, enjoying the rush of warmth that instantly envelops him from the neck down.

Rejoining Lucie, he can make her out better in the glow of the outdoor light she has just turned on. He wants to tell her about what's happening to him, about the blessing that has entered his life, about a gaze so green and limpid and so prodigiously beautiful that it eclipses the world. But Lucie really isn't her usual self.

"What's the matter?"

She seems totally disheartened. Not on the verge of tears, but wrapped in a torpor that drains the colour from life. The rain and darkness are upon her.

"It was a really strange day. Maybe it's the heat ... How about you? Were you too hot? Did you go into the city?"

"Yes, but ... it's funny, I didn't think about the heat."

"You don't say! It's cooler here, by the river, under the trees, than it is anywhere else, but it felt so heavy, all day long. Maybe it's because of what happened ..."

"What?"

"Bah! Things ... First, the priest. He came to give me a lecture this morning. He's claiming that the mayor wants to have us thrown out, that we're a disgrace to the town. They're all the same, our so-called benefactors. Him, too, the priest — he'd like to see us gone. But I've got him, anyway."

"How's that?"

"Bah ... I've got a hold on him. There's a limit to how much poor people will let themselves be laughed at. But that's not the worst of it. Corinne ... (A sob breaks the stream of confidences.) Corinne nearly drowned — God, it was close! The poor thing! Imagine ... A few more seconds and we'd have been too late."

"She went swimming by herself?"

"I don't know what happened. She'd been wearing her bathing suit since this morning, because of the heat. Maybe she wanted to cool off. The other children saw her as she was floating, and I grabbed her just as she was about to go down. It took me at least ten minutes to revive her. It was like she was dead. Poor little corpse! Just like porcelain, that child! She was white, white! I haven't been able to get a word out of her since she came to. She's in shock, I guess. Oh, Étienne, you know what I think? That she hasn't gotten used to her new family, that she's unhappy here. She keeps everything inside, and I don't know how to coax it out. I took her and her little brother in, I try to give her everything she needs. What else can I do?"

"It's true, she has problems," acknowledges Étienne, surprised at the sound of his own voice, an adult voice, imbued with wisdom.

"Problems" is a word that is used by priests and counsellors. Lucie sometimes uses it to demonstrate her superiority over a neighbour, well-heeled but afflicted with behaviour problems, like pathological shyness, or drunkenness: poor Mr. So-and-so, he's got problems …

"And then, to top it all off, dear Gervais comes driving up in an old clunker that belongs to his friend Denis — you know, the fat one — and then gets himself arrested after he crashes into a town councillor's car, Garon, the one who's always been against us."

"Was he hurt?"

"Thankfully, no one was hurt. There were six of them in the car! Aside from that fat Denis, there was Bernadette, Frédérique, Fernand, and Vincent. In spite of the fact that I forbade Gervais to let his sisters and brothers get in the car. Obviously, I might as well be talking to a wall. Those kids do exactly what they please, and what I say just doesn't matter. They probably think I'm babbling, or that I'm just out to bug them. Well! In any case, at least they came out of it unscathed. Except Fernand had a tantrum, as well he might … Garon's car — his beautiful car, almost brand new — was parked near the church. Gervais made a wrong move and ran right into the car. He smashed up the side completely. It looks like it's going to cost a lot to fix it, and on the phone Garon said that this won't be the end of it. Tell me, couldn't Gervais have picked some other car to smash up? That Garon is a real pain. Any time our name has come up at city hall, he's been very hostile. I don't know what we ever did to him to deserve this, but ..."

"And Gervais? Where is he?"

"He's at the police station, at least for tonight. That's what takes the cake. In jail, like a criminal!"

"Is he going to end up with a record?"

"I don't know. No. He's sixteen. I don't think so. And it was just carelessness, nothing more."

"We're going to be paying for that carelessness for a long time."

"There goes some more of Papa's legacy."

The legacy, which Lucie can't dispose of as she sees fit, is a trust account for extraordinary expenses, like repairs to the house.

"Poor Mom! Don't worry, I'll look for a job, and we'll get through this."

"A job! We're in the middle of a recession, my dear. There isn't a job to be found. And if there was, who do you think they'd hire first? The son of that crazy Tourangeau broad?"

"Come on, don't say that!" He smiles at her, touched, and puts his hand on her shoulder again, clasping his bathrobe closed with his other fist. "You know you're the best mom in the world!"

"You're sweet," she says, resting her head against him. "And how was your day? You seem different, somehow."

"What, I'm not usually sweet?" he teases.

"You're always sweet, but it's not always so obvious! Give me something else to think about. Tell me about your day. Did you have fun, at least?"

"Mom, I ... I have some big news ..."

The rain, quiet and very even, falls before them, into the endless distance, to the ends of the world. Lit by the yellow bulb over the entryway, tufts of grass gleam beyond the wooden platform onto which the doors to both apartments open, upstairs and downstairs. Lucie hasn't moved, but it's as if utter misery or happiness waited, crouching in the dark, to pounce on her.

"Mom, on the train this morning, I met someone ... a girl."

"A girl?"

"Her name is Odile."

"Odile!"

The news rises, surges in her, and soon she can't hold it in anymore, squealing, laughing. "Odile?" she says, laughing, and launches herself at him, jostling him, tickling him, undoing his robe while he fights her off, laughing; they're like two loving children, playing at life in the rain, and she teases him, sobbing out repeatedly, "Odile! Odile!" as an odd flash of lightning rends the darkness.

Part II

13

There, in the transparent, generous light, there, that beautiful sweet face, those eyes, so gentle and black, and lips that smile, evanescent. He is shadow made light, his presence is a thin film stretched over the void and, breached, it fades, little by little. There's no way to hold on to it, to keep it, and it vanishes. Odile wakes up. Why is her joy being taken from her? For a moment, she's unhappy, then the truth comes back to her. She smiles. The joy was him. He was in her dream. He slept within her, nested in her thoughts, he inhabits her. Forever. As he vanishes from the dream, he returns as a memory, more handsome still, better. My savage prince. Furtively, she imagines his nakedness, her body instantly vibrating like a sharply strummed harp, and, in particular, she imagines a fire of dark hair above a member that she does not know how to picture.

She'll do what her friends do and buy some condoms.

And he'll come inside her, rejoice in her. And her joy will enclose his, surround his effluence, his milk poured out like blood. The two will make love, create one single love of bodies and souls.

Ah! Delicious sense of well-being! Lying on her back, her hair fanning softly around her head, the sheet drawn up to her neck, Odile lets herself sink and drift in the cool morning air. How pure it is, how clean! Through the open window she hears the chirping of sparrows, mingling with the raucous cries of the mynahs. The thick aroma of peonies floats in, carried by the light breeze that caresses her cheeks.

Yet a worry leaps to mind. Shortly after Étienne left last night, there was a big storm, and it took her several hours to calm down. She pictured her beloved alone, huddled in a makeshift shelter, waiting for the bad weather to pass. How she would have welcomed him into her bedroom and protected him from violence of the night!

She pushes the sheet back, and the light chill bathes her like clear water. Étienne is there, on her, covering her like a sky. He is a field of white and blue air, wrapping her in his smiles, and with her hands she moulds him into the shape of a man. She smoothes his wings, his sides. She presses his hips. He presses in her, on her, centre to centre, awes her.

The sweet aroma of her breasts. She is fragrant with morning, open to a man's joy. Suddenly, she pictures the brandished member clearly, enormous, a drop of clear resin between the two tiny lips. Where has she seen the Object revealed before? It was in that dreadful magazine, forgotten on a park bench, or maybe left there on purpose. It lay open to this intensely inde-cent image. At first she was shocked, then her curiosity over-came her. She looked deliberately at that mass, at its clean lines, delicately nuanced colours, and had seen beauty beneath its apparent grotesqueness. The beauty of life, straightforward as a punch. So vibrant that it silenced the protests of good taste and modesty.

In bed, she contemplates what she can expect from life. Yes, a man will take her absolutely, will crush her with utter pleasure, and will be give her life meaning, direction, a centre; he will make his way in her, as she will in him, will be in her and through her a world to conquer, to expand to the limits of reality. And perhaps, together, they will be God, inhabit the universe to the most distant galaxies, star clusters, to the dawn of time. They will be God and Goddess, entwined, naked, supreme!

It seems to her that the morning's superabundant light and the fricassee of bird songs are intimately linked to her body, and, from within, she senses its beauty, made more radiant by the first flow of desire. At last she understands what sensuality means. Until now, she had not really believed she had the predisposition for it. Sensuality is when the whole body rushes toward the joy of taking and giving, toward the soul to be captured with bare hands. And from that moment on, the body becomes the only wisdom, the only power. It replaces gods and laws, the dogma of learning. The century's great artists, great men and women, are not those who conquer their passion, but those who have discovered, in an embrace, how to live to the fullest. Everything is love, love. Her fingers brush her breasts' hard tips, as in a game, and slide over the slightly flattened globes.

One-thirty! How will she live until then? Their first rendezvous. She'll have to borrow the car or ask for a lift. She'll bring her golf bag, store it in a locker. They'll go walking, just like they did yesterday, but this time the river will be their confidante. He told her about the riverbanks, about the places where his childhood lay in wait. She pictures him as a lively ragamuffin, hiding in the bushes or conjuring up some magic. He must have been a touching sight, with his skimpy garments torn by brambles and bristling with burrs, his black hair in his black eyes, his slender Mohawk snout. A savage among the reeds. But she prefers him with his manly size, his beautiful open hands, the straight smile that reveals his teeth a little, the head where childhood and maturity meet, exchange their mysteries and joys.

A head that belongs to a young man who is intelligent, but impervious to school disciplines because they are so remote from what gives life its honour and joy. Yet Odile believes he could quickly make up for lost time if he put his mind to it. And, when they were talking about their plans, he promised that he'd finish Cegep. When she told him that she'd enrolled in law school, following in her father's footsteps, his handsome face had darkened, and he admitted that he was afraid of losing the respect of someone with so much education, and of not being on a par with her future classmates. She reassured him then, commending his strength of character, which she discerned in everything he told her about his past and which was worth more than any amount of learning; it was, what's more, the foundation of personal development. He'd choose a profession that suited him, become a forest engineer, for example.

"Or an oceanographer?" sighed Étienne, with a timid smile, and he talked at length about a television show he'd seen three years earlier that had made him dream of such a future.

"Well, my prince, anything is possible," she told him.

To that, he replied, "One of my grandfathers was a doctor. Before he immigrated to Canada, my other grandfather was a university professor in Holland. But my dad never finished grade ten, and my mother … Well, let's just say she's self-taught. As you can see, in our family, education tends to drop off."

"There's nothing irreversible about that …"

Today she's going to hammer it home, help him to take himself in hand. Salvation will come to him through her. Isn't anything possible for a young man with talent and guts? And, if he loves, won't he be able to move mountains? Yes, she'll help him, push him along the road to success. Together, they will shape destiny to their desire. Their desire! From the flame of their bodies she will create their home, rooted in life, built on rock, a dense shower of sparks scattering light far and wide, a flame inhabited. Transform the rage of passion that devours them into a will to climb to the summit of life, each through the other.

She stretches with a long sigh, fists closed, twisting the torso whose charms she has suddenly discovered, opens her legs to the beautiful fantasy that assails her and fills her with its hot excess. Her fingers seek a rhythm, barely brushing the edge of her nest of hair, and she dreams of a gentle collision of flesh, while through wet lashes she glimpses the shadows of leaves fluttering on the pale green wall. The morning breeze, laden with aromas and the drone of a solemn horsefly, helps bring forth a joy so keen and sudden that she bites off the scream on her lips and struggles at length with the powerful azure warrior.

14

As soon as he wakes up, Étienne puts on the old bathrobe and goes down the stairs without making a sound. Outdoors, he heads blithely toward the river, strips off the garment, and, blatantly naked, enters the cold water. He hardly slept at all last night, made wakeful by the enormous upheaval in his life, by the incredible luck of this loving, loveable face suddenly taking root in his life, fitting into it as if his entire youth had created the mould for it beforehand. He discussed his various moods with Odile for much of the night, showing her every nook and cranny of his soul, opening himself to her completely, and with this his love was forever strengthened. He wants to live as one naked from now on, as naked as he is in the black water of morning, always to be under his love's eyes, as in his long waking dream, safe from pretense and evasion, offered like a young virgin, protected only by the weapons of desire.

Limbs splashing in the great affectionate ferment, he imagines himself as a girl, penetrated by the force of the water that rises from the abyss, transmits its faint vibration to his entrails, passes completely through him. It's marvellous to be the other sex like this, to be both the sexes, to nourish his virility with the universal sexual drive that has neither direction nor bar. To love Odile, he has to be her as profoundly as possible and thus seem to her like the other part of self, with hard flesh and raised fist, the labarum of an orgasm drawn from her own depths. He in her, she in him, they will tremble, the world will rise in their single body like a sun setting space ablaze, they will tremble in joy exchanged, in parts dispersed, she will be his penis, and he will burst open with her great vagina laugh, and their seed will flow out, reaching the night's low branches. He laughs, water bathing his teeth, then plunges his head into the water and remains still for a long time, drowning in the exhilaration of love; he drowns the fatigue gathered in his eyes, laughs, laughs in the water, pretends to be drowned, lets himself be taken by the powerful call of the depths where, legs wide, the carnal lover awaits him, flesh of flesh. Then, nearly suffocating, he pulls himself together with a start, and rises up to the magic of the fair morning.

Enough fooling around. To build love, it takes a clear head, not a languishing soul. To keep Odile's love, thinks Étienne, I have to be worthy of her. Worthy! And that means no more lazing around, no more petty, arid regrets, no more short-sightedness. The future is a dream that has to be dreamed magnificently, like a great house to be furnished with our vows and brought into our life with the splendour of youth fulfilled. To be young, to achieve! Together create our lives with all our strength, maddened with work and success, to build our relationship by focusing on our professions, our achievements growing before our eyes. Then, when evening comes, leave work behind and make love together, my joy in you, my hands clasping your shoulders, my hard penis in you blessing our rhythms, our blood, and you overcome, surging over me with your great golden pleasure, a tide of fire, a soul delighted!

But before that, before a lifetime of love in their own house, there is education to be acquired, separately, at least for now. Maybe in a year or two they'll be able to rent an apartment together near the university. Until then, they'll have to be apart most of the time, maybe meeting on the sly, without Odile's parents finding out in case they don't see him as a desirable catch. Étienne doesn't underestimate the difficulties that could arise from that corner. Yet, isn't the amazing thing that he loves; that she exists; that at first glance their minds recognized each other and intertwined; that, from within their deepest and most passionate selves, their bodies call to each other? He loves! Nothing so magnificent has happened to him since that day he has sometimes heard about when he entered life from between the thighs of a young adorable mother, hot with sleep and blood, ready for the adventures belonging to a new individual among the myriad individualities of past and present. Becoming one, one self among so many others, striking a balance among the plethora of destinies by claiming his rightful share of tragedy and happiness, worthy of living among the men and women of this world, of mingling his breath with the breath of a being like himself, of merging his gaze with the light and clarity of her gaze. Becoming love that is the grand immersion in the other, in which the self is found through losing itself, being born to the other and to oneself, this is what love is at twenty, what has given Étienne back the glorious nakedness of the child.

Swimming calmly above the abyss, he watches the blue house reflecting in the water's folds, basking in a blaze of foliage. From his point of view, and in his state of mind, the house and yard strike Étienne as almost entirely charming, utterly charming. But at length some familiar details creep into his awareness and irritate him. What a mess! How is it that the general dilapidation, the neglected grass, the heaps of garbage do not bother his mother who, in spite of how weird she looks, is very sensitive? Étienne remembers when they arrived at the new house three years ago, the flawless magic of the place, the fiery snakes of light cast on the veranda by the calm water. For one whole morning, he watched gyrating tadpoles and squadrons of minnows veering toward indiscernible objectives, red and blue dragonflies perching on water lilies. All was bright, and the laughs, the yells kept harmony with the beauty. Unfortunately, it only took a few days before satisfaction degenerated into sloppiness and devastation.

A lawnmower was deemed an unnecessary expense. To Lucie, letting the grass grow as it would seemed preferable to the monotony of a well-tended lawn. Then the dandelions, the goldenrod, the chicory would arrive to delight the eyes. Manicured lawns are like overeducated people, cursed by the ridiculous formalities of their status. Long live youth and its salubrious ignorance!

And, in this enchanting setting, they had gone back to their gay and carefree ways without worrying about the property's rapid deterioration, helped along in great part by Fernand's rages. Why put back the torn off shutters? He'll destroy them as soon as he can. Better to leave them where they are, as if to remind his demons that their demolition work is already done. As for the other children, they made the best of the law of least action adopted by their mother, indolent and overwhelmed by her chores. Only Marie-Laure and Frédérique would help her at mealtime; the others were usually exempted from chores.

This morning, using a minimum of motion to keep himself upright in the water and looking at the riverbank, Étienne feels a fierce determination invading him. If he wants to bring Odile home, introduce her to his mother, his sisters and brothers, if he wants to give the girl he loves a proper welcome, he will have to evict squalor, throw poorhouse sloppiness out, give the blue house back its song-like freshness. This will be the first step he takes toward a future that is in keeping with his love. He will restore dignity to everything, to dear Lucie, bowing under her burdens, to the entire chorus of lives for which he, the eldest, now feels responsible. He will be the man of this house, the one it has never had, even and especially when Chonchon pastured his impenetrable dreams amidst the family's racket.

As the idea takes hold of him, he starts to caress his left arm beneath the slightly oily, almost soapy water. He washes himself with his bare hand, eradicates the grime from his skin, going to each of his limbs one by one, then scrubbing his chest, cleaning himself with his two urgent, patient hands, ending with his face, which he washes meticulously with the tips of his fingers. After his ablutions, carried out while swimming in place near the large eddies, he feels the fatigue of a too-short night lifting, the fatigue of a night spent dreaming with open eyes, then visited by biting nightmares about being once more caught in the storm. He emerges from the water, nonchalantly dons the bathrobe that doesn't close, observes, amused, a neighbour's grey head at her window, doesn't bother to toss her an insult. He heads for the front of the house to go back to his bedroom. There, he finds Gervais half slumped on the wooden platform with his back to the wall, looking very unlike his usual happy-go-lucky self. Then Étienne thinks of his mother, whom he found in a similar position a few hours earlier.

"You're here?" he says, sitting by his side.

Gervais doesn't answer. This morning, his smiling ferret's face is so closed and ashen that he's almost unrecognizable. Étienne doesn't know what to say and he puts his hand on Gervais's shoulder, as he did with Lucie.

"Don't touch me. Don't touch me!" And Gervais suddenly bursts into tears, unable to contain his anguish, and something like little whimpers can be heard through the sobs.

"What's the matter, little brother? What did they do to you?"

"Don't touch me, I never want to be touched again. I don't! I don't!"

"Did they beat you?"

To escape from the unwanted solicitude, Gervais gets up and opens the door to the first floor. Étienne notices that he's having trouble walking. A kind of brown shadow stains his jeans between the legs, as if Gervais had been bleeding.

15

"You're a disgrace, madam, a goddamned disgrace! And your children are just like you: they're disgraces too! Have you got that?"

He is facing her, enormous, powerful, scarlet with anger and contempt, his fists on his hips, and he's thundering at her. They can surely hear him five houses away. This will be a real treat for the neighbours. Yesterday, the priest; today, Normand Garon, the municipal councillor in person, come to vent his spleen about the damage done to his car. It's too good an opportunity. For years, this livid man has been clamouring to banish the family that dishonours the town. Lucie lets him pour out his rage. He got here bursting with imprecations and started to rake her down without further ado, hurling insult upon insult at her. She thought about throwing him out instantly, even if she had to wrestle with him, then changed her tactics, hoping to turn the situation to her advantage. And she's too horrified by what's been done to Gervais to let this opportunity for proclaiming her indignation go to waste. The moment is too perfect: this is one person who's going to know what she thinks and, as it happens, this is precisely their most unrelenting persecutor.

As he shouts, she coldly examines the anger intended to intimidate her and which has placed two flat shoes of shining leather on her linoleum, shoes ridiculously deformed by bunions. Under his garishly styled clothing, she pictures his undergarments, his pitiful anatomy. He's a barrel crammed full of arrogance and excrement who talks, acts, breathes in the name of the respect he's owed because never, since he set foot on this earth, has he dreamed that he could be treated any other way or that he could have to earn the consideration he revels in.

"We're going to drive you out, my dear lady, you and your tribe of badly brought up children who are a disgrace to this town. You can go and set up your goddamned pigsty somewhere else, since you can't live like a normal person! You're a pig, the daughter of a savage, you've never known a thing about cleanliness or proper behaviour. You should be living in a shack out on the edge of a field so your kids can run around naked, like animals, and you can, too! Your neighbours are all complaining about your scandalous ways; they often see those grown-up boys of yours going getting into the water with nothing on, and as for you, we all know what this house turns into every night! It's a disgrace! And you just stand there looking at me without turning a hair, as if I were talking Iroquois — Oh, no, that's right, that you would understand!"

"I understand what you're saying, sir."

Lucie's calm tone disconcerts the seething dignitary for a second. His face, relaxed now, looks like a crêpe, hanging in soft folds. His little grey eyes shine like slugs between his puffy eyelids.

"I understand what you're saying perfectly," she continues. "You want to get rid of us because, rather than shaving my lawn and letting it be scorched by the sun, like all my neighbours do, like you do yourself, I let nature take its course. My lawn isn't already yellow as soon as June rolls around, and it has pretty flowers, too. That's environmentally friendly, as they say. But I don't expect to convert you to my way of doing things. The main thing that bugs you is that I bring my children up in an atmosphere of freedom; I teach them that happiness is the most important thing to look for, not wealth and glory. My children don't care about money. They're happy with what little they've got, that's what outrages you. As for their manner of living, sir, well, rest assured that it is wholesome, which is more than I can say for what goes on in your perfect little world. My son Gervais, sir, was thrown in jail yesterday, which must have really made you happy, and this morning he came home to me covered in blood and tears because the cops spent the whole night raping him, do you hear me? Do you understand? Am I talking Iroquois now? That's your perfect middle-class world. Tidy lawns, well-kept homes, but behind the façades there is such filth, it is so utterly sickening that it makes me want to vomit! And you, sir, are a party to it, a party to this abomination!"

"What you're saying ... that the police raped ... it's probably not true. I'm going to check ..."

"Not true? Not true! You've got some nerve! Do I have to show you his ass? Do you want to put your finger in the hole, like Thomas?"

"Have a little dignity, madam! If you're so sure of yourself, you should just file a complaint in court."

"Oh, that's a really good one! A complaint against the police! That would really suit you: that would get us out of here in no time. The courts! Perhaps you think they're there to protect the rights of poor people?"

"In any case, that's what happens when children are allowed to do exactly what they please. My children, madam, don't wind up in jail."

"True enough — it's pretty unlikely that they'd ever get arrested, and less likely still that they'd be treated like a piece of meat. Those who have the power have all the privileges. Only poor people get the attention of the justice system. As for the police! Those bastards! If I run into the ones who attacked my son, I'll ..."

"Better be careful what you say! Threats can cost you."

"You're a real piece of work! Not only don't you care about what's been done to a poor boy, but you're even taking away my right to protest it. You must really hate the poor! What, you don't even have one iota of Christian charity toward a destitute neighbour?"

"Charity! Charity! Start by earning it, inject a few manners into your gang of brats, then we'll have something to talk about. I've had enough of your jeremiads, madam! As for your goddamned little bastards, you'd better keep them home! You've been warned!"

The big man pushes the door open, letting it slam behind him, but finds himself face to face with Étienne, who is determined to block his path.

"Get out of my way, you little snot!"

He tries to jostle the young man, who stands fast.

"It's revolting, what you did to my brother!"

"I didn't lay a finger on your brother." He lets out a crude laugh. "What do you think I am, a fag?"

"No, you're something much worse than that. You've been hounding us for years, just for the pleasure of causing trouble. But even if you didn't actually lay your dirty paws on my brother, you know exactly what goes on at the police station. Scum like you, well, we don't see that too often!"

In a rage, the dignitary slaps Étienne, who continues to stare at him coldly while Lucie, who's been listening to the flare-up, comes to her son's rescue.

"If you touch my son again, you'll have to answer to me."

"Well, look at the bitch protecting her little mongrel! You goddamned squaw! You're a real sight! Ooh! I'm scared! The lady doesn't want me to hurt her worthless deadbeat wimp of a son!"

Without warning, he launches a vicious kick that catches Étienne under the kneecap. Étienne can't hold back a moan. He retaliates with a solid slap to his assailant's face, and Garon's nose starts to bleed.

"You little swine, you're going to regret that!"

With his nose in a handkerchief, the councillor wheels around and gets back to his car, on which the marks of the accident are plain. His stormy departure fills the air with a long, dusty shriek.

16

"I'll be back in a minute."

Odile opens the car door, glancing at her mother's profile — impenetrable, as always — out of the corner of her eye, gets out, and, with small, graceful steps, enters the drugstore. She spots the magazine rack, rummages through the stacks of myriad publications, primarily American, and finds the one she's looking for. She brings it to the counter, but, as she passes by the display of contraceptives, she furtively grabs a small, appealing box and places it, blushing, before the salesgirl. The latter, with the impassiveness of the true professional, rings up the sale and gives her the change. Before she departs, Odile opens the bag and slips the small box into the pouch attached to her belt.

"Here, I found it. This was the last one," she tells her mother, throwing the magazine onto the back seat.

"It must be quite tattered, then."

"No, not really."

Mrs. Louvier shifts into gear with slow deliberation, and the powerful car rolls forward, silently.

"How long do you think the game will last?"

"I don't know. Don't worry, I'll find my own way home. Maybe someone will offer me a lift, or I'll take a taxi."

"Will you be home for supper?"

"Yes ... unless something comes up. If that happens, I'll call you."

Silence falls as the vehicle glides in front of opulent villas, with the abstract perfection of a long tracking shot. From this kind of passenger compartment, with its lightly tinted windows, life seems to roll by like a movie, a colour film, but silent, since the noise from the exterior is muted. The air conditioning makes only a slight murmur, almost a whisper.

"How about you, Mom? Do you have a very busy day today, as usual?"

"Bah! I've a few errands to run. Then I'm seeing Luce, as usual. We might go to the movies."

"And how is Aunt Luce?"

"Wonderful! She gets younger every day!"

"Widowhood has made a new woman of her. It's remarkable."

"Hush! Don't talk like that. Poor Raymond!"

"Yeah!"

They share a harmless, knowing laugh.

"Oh, here's the golf course. I envy you: what a beautiful, sunny afternoon! You're sure you won't be too hot?"

"There's a nice breeze. And I've got my horrible little hat, if the sun's too strong."

"I'll open the trunk for you."

Odile takes out her clubs, returns to give her mother a kiss, then heads for the clubhouse, pulling the cart behind her. She and Étienne have arranged to meet inside to avoid any surprises. Moving from bright daylight into a large, poorly lit room, she has to stop to let her eyes adjust to the dimness. Aside from the fat girl behind the counter, she can only make out four golfers, who are seated at a table with drinks in front of them. Uncertain, she moves to the counter. The girl smiles broadly at her.

"Do you want to sign up for a round?"

"No ... I'm meeting someone ... do you know Étienne Tourangeau?"

"Étienne!"

The name, uttered with a note of incredulity, seems to slip out of the heavy girl. Odile is astonished to see her turn crimson and lose her friendly air. The clerk pulls herself together, however, murmuring, "No, I haven't seen him today. He was here yesterday morning. You say you have an appointment?"

"Yes, at one-thirty, that is ... now. I'm sure he won't be long ..."

"Boys, you know, you shouldn't count on them too much," says the girl, oddly vehement, with renewed but ambiguous helpfulness.

Odile moves toward the window. The golfers have noticed her and, with clumsy gallantry, invite her to join them. She turns her back to them. They broadcast their disappointment loudly, then go back to discussing the relative merits of Japanese and American cars.

Love is such a busy craftsman of future possibilities that the slightest refutation by reality causes incredible catastrophes to leap to mind. Since she awoke, Odile has been buoyed up by feverish anticipation of the moment that will return Étienne to her. Now, she doesn't understand why he's not here, by one-forty, as if punctuality didn't matter to the young man, doesn't understand how anything, no matter how serious, could jeopardize their encounter. She finally sees him, running as fast as he can, like a kid, and joy surges into her once more. It doesn't take him long to reach her. His chest is heaving, his quickened breath mingles with hers.

"I'm sorry," he says, cutting short his kiss. "I ran as hard as I could to keep you from waiting too long. I was held up at home ..."

She contemplates him, in a tight yellow shirt and dark blue jeans that emphasize his limbs' harmony. His careless attire shows off his natural elegance. It doesn't take him long to catch his breath. Drawing Odile to him once more, he smiles. "Now we can kiss. Hello, Odile!"

She offers him her lips, quivering as his mouth touches her, then pulls back herself.

"Not here ... Let's go outside."

"I'll get them to store your clubs."

He moves away with the cart and addresses Annie. She serves him sternly, her cheeks redder than ever. What, could this fat girl be jealous? he asks himself, astonished. He doesn't linger over on the question and quickly rejoins Odile, leading her outside.

The sky has the deep, absolute blue of days that are not too hot, enlivened by dazzlingly fleecy clouds. Étienne is enjoying the sensation — new to him — of wrapping his arm around a girl's delicious body, a girl who is a fountain of light hair that tumbles in a silk caress, an incredible caress on his forearm, who is a loving, lovable face, whose features are a poem, a blessing. Happiness flows back to him from her, a spontaneous offering of desire that sets their flesh vibrating and blends spirit with flesh, because the soul is all desire and will. Each soul wants the other, entirely, down to the bones, the teeth, the flaming smile.

Tenderly pressed together, they walk toward the entrance to the course, then Étienne leads Odile to the road that runs along the river. The riverbank is drowned in the shade cast by large trees, but further away the rapids foam in the sunlight, and, not far off shore, the island spreads a rippling layer of green under the sun's effusions.

"There's 'my' island," says Étienne, his gesture as emphatic as the owner of a large estate.

"Magnificent, Your Lordship! And how do we get there?"

"There's a way to cross nearby. In the summertime, the water is so low that it only comes to your knees. In the spring, you can't get across; the island's half underwater, anyway."

"The landscape is so beautiful!" Her face clouds. "Earlier, when I saw that you weren't there ..."

He interrupts her, gazing into her eyes, his own full of anguish. "If you only knew, Odile! I swear, I couldn't do anything else. Please forgive me, but you've got to understand ... I'll tell you what happened."

"No, I'm not blaming you for anything. I just want you to know how the thought of never seeing you again — you get crazy at a time like that! You always imagine the worst — it just tore me apart, all of a sudden! My sweet Étienne!"

She gently strokes his arm, covered with fine dark hair, then places her lips on it. Next to her, he feels tall and wise and forthright; he knows the future doesn't exist any more than the past does, that there is only the present, this walk, side by side, the secrets of the island to raise in wild flights beneath their footsteps. He feels so good next to that other self, unknown and yet allied with him, in tune with all his desires and shames! As if by instinct, he senses what caresses his large nimble hand could venture through the bouquets of inhibition and the fires of excitement, what kisses he could plant in these furrows of soft flesh, and what glances he could let fall, like celestial butterflies, on the happy accidents that are her flesh, features, gestures, sighs. First holding her at arm's length, in her young woman's remoteness, in friendship, then possessing her, in her gentle sweetness, to be her young and ravished master. Let her be my blessing, my life!

Once on the grey pebble bank, they take off their shoes and roll up their pant legs. Round stones, sand nesting between them, cover the partly exposed bed. Here and there, branches, caught and scoured by the current, shed the yellow-brown sheen of old bones.

"Did you see that?" exclaims Étienne. "A pickerel!"

"Where?"

"It just went past that big rock."

She presses against him, asking, in a nervous voice, "Are you sure it's safe?"

"Of course it is. I told you, the water doesn't go past your knees and the current's not strong on this side of the island, you know. And, I'm going to hold onto you."

"I know ... but what about the fish? What if they attack us?"

In the sunshine, Étienne's laugh is so beautiful that Odile instantly abandons fear and, on an impulse, she decides, "Let's go!"

Positioned upstream, as if to break the current, Étienne grips Odile sturdily with his hand on her hip and shows her which stones to step on. Soon, they're soon stepping onto the island. Then Étienne takes her in his arms and whispers tenderly, "You see, it was perfectly safe."

She smiles, an expectant smile, and onto her smile the young man places his lips, at first very soft, barely brushing, a mere breath. Then their lips speak to each other, speak love in kisses that create night around them at midday, make a bedroom under the high branches, spread out walls of silk, envelop them in a muffled coolness. Gradually, their hearts soaring, they progress through the naked country of the other's dreams, invent the weapons of their delight, mingle their astounding beauty, arm to arm, belly to belly, and the radiance of their sexuality strikes their bodies endlessly, for the first time, that time of all times, leaving them half-dead with pleasure and emotion.

They remain entwined, naked, for a long time. They are sacred guardians: her breasts radiating such innocence that they burn the shadows, his still-swollen member labouring with unappeasable excitement. Around them, life has begun anew, clusters of leaves lash in the wind, dividing the azure sky into small, cold sparks, and the powerful trunks stand guard against bad luck. It is an enchanted wood, where everything lives and thrives so that, in their bodies, a single soul of bright flame can bloom.

17

Good God! thinks Lucie. I have to get rid of some of these clothes. There's no room to walk.

She has just entered the boys' room, where she has not ventured for several weeks. For her, the room is her men's sacred refuge, and they are free to deal with it as they see fit. If they loathe cleaning up, too bad for them. Or so much the better, order being the most sterile of middle-class virtues. She gets her superb contempt for the commandments of cleanliness and tidiness from her Amerindian forebears, Lucie believes. She knows instinctively that it's better to cope with garbage than to relegate it to the outside world, where, with the municipality's blessing, it will eventually haunt everybody. Aren't the dumps poisoning the groundwater? Don't sewers pollute the streams and rivers? And, far from being annoyed, Lucie looks kindly upon the piles of clothes and miscellany that, in the boys' room, grow far larger than they do elsewhere in the house. Boys, at least, should not be asked to worship the domestic virtues.

She carries a brimming bowl of cereal and keeps her balance with enormous difficulty as she makes her way to the bed where Gervais lies sleeping. It's about two o'clock in the afternoon. The sun casts a blinding square of light in the middle of the floor, and it reflects throughout the room.

She puts the bowl on the floor, sits down next to her child, who is curled up like a puppy, naked, his face streaked with tears. His sleep is tense, and he suddenly lets out a moan. She hesitates, wondering if she should tear him from his nightmares, then puts her hand on his shoulder. He starts, looks at her for a moment, then says, weakly, "Mom."

"Good morning, sweetheart. How are you feeling today?"

He doesn't answer. A vague languor freezes his green eyes, which hold none of their usual malice. She caresses his thin arm, saying, "Aren't you cold?"

He huddles into her, and tears spill over once again, great sobs shaking him from head to toe. The contractions of his body wring out other cries of pain.

"It hurts, it hurts!" he cries. "It feels like an iron rod's being pushed into me! It's awful!"

"My poor baby! When you can get up, we'll go to the emergency room."

"No. There's nothing they can do."

"Why do you say that? I'm sure the doctors will be able to ease the pain."

For a moment, he says nothing, then replies grimly, "No. I know. It just has to get better on its own."

There are things she senses but refuses to look at more closely. The moment's ills are sufficient, and there's nothing to be achieved by going after further revelations.

"I brought you some cereal. Are you hungry?"

"No. Yes. I'll eat something in a little while."

"You need your strength."

After a few more stabs of pain make Gervais grit his teeth,

he seems to calm down a little. Suddenly shivering, he realizes that he's naked and tries to cover up, but the sheet is wound into a ball and he's unable to draw it over himself.

"Don't worry, my darling Gervais," murmurs Lucie, "I've seen you naked before. I brought you into this world, remember?"

"You brought me into this world, and all this sex filth, you made me from your shit, fucking whore, you made me a whore like you, goddamned mother of shit! Get lost, I want to be alone! Get it? Go away! I don't want to see anybody, for Christ's sake!"

18

His back propped on a folded pillow, Chonchon sprawls on the bed in front of the television, watching Vanessa's latest video. Bottle in hand, he's wallowing in an odd mood, a blend of resentment and indulgence. When he watches these epitomes of manhood occupying the divine receptacles, pushing their way into that smiling, clearly welcoming, in fact, beckoning mouth, or plunging into the body's moist disorder, sometimes assailing the forbidden orifice, icy beads of jealous perspiration cover his forehead. Fists clenched, limbs stiffened against the onslaught of shame, he is forced to conquer the painful feelings that surge up, one by one, from childhood: the fear of hell, a conviction that he's been damned for accepting the degeneracy in which he now rots, then a desire to become as pure as he once was, until teenage masturbation forever severed him from his original innocence. Most of all, there's a burning feeling of inferiority in matters of copulation: he gave his wife seven children and perhaps never satisfied her even once. Only with Vanessa has he found a sexuality in tune with his own, always ready and quickly spent. Certainly, with her, he almost always tastes the pride of shared bliss, but he knows she's too fervent for their brief raptures to satisfy her. The video series came to her rescue, giving her a professional pretext for peccadilloes that were inevitable anyway, not to mention the extra cash that comes in handy at the end of the month. During a recession, even extravagance, no matter how cuddly, sells poorly, and Chonchon was quick to see the advantages of tapping a very natural resource — always in demand — like this incredible piece of womanhood. It was Vanessa's own idea. She told him about a cousin she'd met recently who'd offered her a role in a small production. She sold him on the idea that the pay was good, the role was small, not exactly prim — in fact, completely nude — and he slapped her once or twice, half-heartedly, before agreeing to it: "Yes, my pet, it's necessary." But he demanded to see the results, so as not to be played for a fool, and since then has fumed through each new performance. They last fifteen awful minutes, during which she leaves the room, coming back to him when they're over, when he's humiliated and burning for relief.

Today's selection is a domestic comedy with a particularly idiotic title: *Flowers in the Tooth Glass*. After being duly relieved of his morning tumescence by his wife, a husband runs off to work. Instantly, bearing a nice bouquet, her lover comes to the back door. The wife absentmindedly tosses the flowers into the glass by the bedside. The glass contains something pink — dentures! The two luscious bodies engage in lengthy and edifying frolics. Methodically, they try out a wide variety of positions; both appear to delight in stimulating the other. Suddenly, the husband shows up: he's forgotten his dentures. How incredibly surprised he is! Then angry! Then magnanimous, for he's broadminded: he loves his wife and really doesn't want to drive her away. Handshaking and hugs all around. Dentures in place, the husband shows what he is capable of, and a healthy competition ensues, all for the greater enjoyment of the one on the receiving end.

And now the door swings open once more. Shyly, a very young, incredibly handsome man enters, wielding a feather duster. It's the housekeeper. He's come to get his orders from the lady of the house, and doesn't immediately realize how ill-timed his entrance is. The lady leaps on the opportunity and has no trouble gaining his consent. The young stud soon finds himself suitably dressed and wielding a different implement, one that makes his colleagues pale with envy. And Chonchon also writhes with pain: Vanessa never said a word to him about this particular cousin, obviously afraid of what he would say. Because he could be her son: he doesn't even look eighteen. What a beautiful boy! Now that really bothers Chonchon. As long as they kept to the usual porn encounters between people of the same kidney, played by the rules, it was no big deal. But adding perversion to sex, no matter how graceful, now that is far too risky. Plus, how is Chonchon supposed to put up with watching his sweetheart besieged by such a beauty? The child is amazing! Though spectacular, his assets are still inherently graceful and brilliant deployed. Worse yet, the other two studs are getting into the game, and the three of them come at Vanessa from all sides. The crowning horror is when the husband's hand wanders between young Ganymede's buttocks. Now that's going too far. There's heterosexuality and homosexuality. Women might, if necessary, strip off their clothes and prime each other for the ecstasy to be delivered by a male — that wouldn't bring down the heavens. In fact, upon reflection, it's only natural. But for a man to develop a taste for other men and seek his pleasure there, that opens the door to the unknown, throws it wide open, especially when the man still claims to have natural desires. How to conceive of such a sharing of the sexes? How to love both a man and a woman without sinking into the worst kind of degeneracy? Although familiar with chimeras, Chonchon's glimpse of the paradox of hybrid flesh repels him. The imagination he uses in his work, for children's pleasure, has woven a few surprises out of nature's somewhat loose mesh, but it rebels against this offence, a man's hand falling now on a quivering nipple, now on a chest adorned with thick golden hair.

The last straw is when Chonchon sees Vanessa, totally enthralled, taking the newcomer's lust in her mouth. She'd sworn not to do anything risky. Does she think she's immune? What proof does she have that that young squire is clean? That's too much! He'll have to throw her out or he could get infected one day. Yes, yes, that's what he'll do, as soon as she shows her face. No more being taken in by her protests of good faith and her words of honour. What filth!

Yet he loves her, in spite of all her sins, he loves her! And she's so sweet when she's not under the spell of her passion for pleasure, or when she focuses her ardent heart on her beloved Chonchon, her fractious Chonchon, whose bad moods she can skilfully remove, one by one, as if she were changing a baby's diapers. Yes, she mothers him, she is a sweet mother with luscious lips, thick with a red that is almost orange, a small nose like a scamp's, or like a shell with nostrils scrolling down into mother-of-pearl, and soulless eyes, green as gaiety, exuberance, a cordial absence of thought.

But this sweetheart gives herself to others, to all others, takes her pleasure from the first man to come along, courts infection, flirts with the most degrading of deaths! She risks her life, along with her partner's — the one who's always been so good to her — for the pleasure of communing with the raw beauty of a soul, of swallowing the terrible seed that is the origin of life. Suddenly, Chonchon is shattered, and tears of gin slide down his pathetic cheeks, his chest heaving with authentic sobs. His sobs mingle with the telephone's howls, and at first he can't tell them apart. Finally, the ringing brings him back to earth, and he sniffs for a minute, then picks up the receiver.

"Hello, Chonchon?"

The overly melodious voice hits him like a slap, and he's tempted to hang up. It's too much, in the middle of his drunkenness, his sorrow, his malign passion, to be reconnected with the past, to hear the goodness of that voice, unbearable. Dear Lucie, dear little mother!

"Hello, are you there?"

"Yes, yes. I'm here."

"Good God, it doesn't sound like things are going very well. Am I disturbing you?"

"No ... Wait a second, I'll turn off the TV."

He drops the bottle as he gets up, and gin spills onto the sheets. He swears at length, but manages to save some. He puts the bottle safely on the night table and sullenly picks up the phone.

"Great, that does it. I've just wet my bed, but not with pee. I knocked my bottle over, Christ," he says with a disgusted laugh.

Lucie laughs too, out of politeness, then moves on to serious business. "Chonchon, dear, we haven't talked in a long time. How is everything?"

"Everything's fine, thank you, it could be worse. How are you? The children?"

"That's exactly why I'm calling. Chonchon ... Chonchon, since you left, I haven't bothered you with my domestic problems very often, you can't say I have. Well ... now, I need you. Really!"

Stunned, Chonchon can hear violent sobs coming from the other end of the line. He pulls the receiver away from his ear, waits a minute, then, overcome, asks, "Are things that bad? What's going on, Lulu, darling?"

"I can't take it anymore, Chonchon! I can't take it! It seems like everything's falling apart, everything's turning against me. You know, a home needs a man, a real head of the family. It's important. I can't do everything, I can't meet all their needs. I'm not blaming you for anything, I'm just trying to explain a little. Sometimes, the fact that you're not here is really hard to handle. Right now, everything's going wrong."

"I understand, Lulu, but you know what it was like at the end. Sometimes, it's harder to deal with someone being there than it is to see them go. What are you asking me for, exactly? You don't want me to come back, do you?"

"No, of course not, I know you need your freedom. But if you could just come over for a few hours, I think that would solve a lot of problems. And it would make the kids so happy!"

"By the way, did Étienne tell you that he dropped by to introduce his girlfriend?"

"Yes! I was so glad that he thought of you in that situation! Oh, he must be feeling so proud, and proud of you, too! As a matter of fact, after he told me, I thought that you might be able to give us a hand, if it's not asking too much. I don't want to keep you from your work, but you could come over in the evening and leave the next morning. Just for a few days, to help us get back on our feet."

"But tell me what's gone wrong. Étienne didn't mention anything."

"There are a lot of things."

She tells him, in a muddled way, about the visits from the priest and the town councillor, Corinne's near drowning, Gervais's mischief, the treatment meted out to the poor boy. Chonchon finds enough horror among the tangled bits and pieces of the tale to turn his troubled feelings, blended with gin and lust, towards indignation.

"Well, expect me for supper, Lulu, I'll be there. You'll see, together, we're going to sort your fucking problems out, and it won't take long, either!"

Lucie's happy exclamations and expressions of advance gratitude sound as if she were hearing the voice of her saviour. Chonchon hangs up the phone, a firm resolution taking hold of him. This is the perfect opportunity to get his life back on track and break away from the creature who's putting him in grave danger. He grabs a notepad and scrawls, with clenched teeth:

My sexy Vanessa,

I saw your last tape. Congratulations! You're getting them real young nowadays! And handsome, too. That one must really have made you come! BITCH!

I've had enough of living dangerously. If you want to die of AIDS, that's your business. But I'm clean. Keep your germs to yourself. I'm no longer going to stand for being dragged through the mud by a whore like you. Take off! GET LOST!

I have to go away for a few days, but I want you to get your stuff out of the house TODAY. Go on, sleep with your young boys, they love old bitches like you in their goddamn putrid beds!

To think I loved you! Never set foot here again.

Chonchon

19

After walking Odile back to the clubhouse, Étienne has retraced his steps to the bridge. He's waiting for the six o'clock train to go by before he starts onto it. A rumbling noise becomes audible, rapidly grows louder, and, at the head of the curve that had hidden it from view, he soon sees the engine's square mass hurtling toward him. Although he's far enough from the tracks, he backs up a little, enduring the driver's menacing glare without flinching. Of course, no one is allowed to walk along the tracks, let alone use the viaduct, but the police never do anything, and all the conductors and railway workers do is bawl out the offenders when they get a chance.

An afternoon devoted to the overwhelming discovery of carnal intimacy has left Étienne with weak knees and a heart full of unutterable delight. Now, with each breath, the vivid memory of a face hovers before him, a face radiant with the sweet pain of love and pulsing with consent. A carnal gift of profound sensuality, a gift of tears and kisses, an entire shuddering self ablaze, kindling stirred in a rain of fire. Odile burns in him, and he, with his arms, with his bundle of bones erected upon the naked earth, flames with a young and beautiful truth that is yet a child's but ripe now for a man's accomplishments.

Limp, emptied, full of love's extraordinary happiness, tousled, with sleep circles shadowing his eyes like blue ash, Étienne waits beside the train. The stop now over, it slowly begins to move. Some of the travellers are looking out the window, absently contemplating the tall pines along the golf course. A green can be seen through a gap, with a few golfers playing onto it. Étienne is watching the train pick up speed when he suddenly hears his name called. From one of the windows, his father gives him a big smile and waves. Étienne waves back, but he's seized by anxiety. Though he can't explain it, this unusual visit seems like a bad sign, under the circumstances.

When Étienne arrives, Chonchon is still busy dealing with the children's outpourings of joy, particularly Fernand's, who aspires to be the favourite. When Chonchon is there, it is understood that the unstable boy is entitled to the greatest share of his attention, which doesn't keep him from being jealous or from having a violent tantrum each time his father goes on his solitary way.

Chonchon has thus been careful to fuss over the most fragile child first. Then he gives way to the intoxication of being fawned over by his daughters, whom he adores, especially the older ones. But he's stunned by Frédérique. She has become a woman since his last visit a few months ago. Her once quite nondescript face has taken on a look of regal beauty, the kind that shines deep in the virgin forest, and he is dumbfounded by it. She's the very image of Lucie! Twenty years ago, when he first met the woman who became his wife, he had been bewitched by the same lustre of night and mystery emanating from a slim body infused with a mute, irresistible sensuality. It was like a boy's ambiguous beauty, except for the deliciously provocative breasts, the tender pelvic curve.

"Well, my little woman, it's amazing how much you look like your mother!" he says, resting his eyes on her.

She smiles, a little confused. His stare is scrutinizing, almost searching, and she can feel Marie-Laure growing jealous while waiting for her share of praise. But Étienne steps in, giving his father a hearty handshake.

"Hello, son! So, you're crossing the train bridge on foot? That's pretty dangerous."

"Yes, but it's free. Danger," he adds, laughing, "is always free."

"Do you remember Ti-Nest Laroche, the one who drowned?"

"Bah! He didn't have much of a head on his shoulders. As for me, I don't even know what vertigo is. And I make sure I never cross when a train's coming."

"Fine. You're old enough to know what you're doing."

Lucie has been silent since Chonchon's arrival, moved by this scene of the father's reunion with his children. Could a celebration be any more magnificent in its simplicity? It's as if the daily order had been suddenly upturned and reorganized around one essential axis. The father! She remembers the old man, her own father — long moments spent with him, replete with silence and affection between the melancholy academic and herself, the child, who couldn't picture a world without that small house full of dusty books, the fireplace with embers shaped like glowing catacombs, an intermittent mother, smiling and distracted, whom her wild imagination placed on shadowy paths. The little girl clung to this pitiable man who, for better or worse, filled in for the vagabond, enveloping the child with distinct, desperate tenderness.

Here, she is the pillar, and her man comes and goes as he pleases. Chonchon has never really been a father. He took refuge in her like a child in his mother's bosom. He gave her all the children she wanted, provided a fairy-tale family for a mother goose who is somewhat of a grasshopper, enjoying herself for the moment. He's enjoying himself, too, and how! But today, she wants to believe that those days are over, that they can get their house into some kind of order. After all, these latest threats are beginning to sound serious, and she won't always be able to fend them off with blackmail of the kind she holds in reserve against that poor priest to whom she showed the moon and stars. Now that her husband is here, she feels a little ashamed at the memory of that fat and pallid flesh. Thank goodness she changed the sheets. Life can get back to normal.

"But where on earth is Gervais?" inquires Chonchon.

"He's lying down, the poor thing," explains Lucie. "He's really shaken up, because …"

"Yes, you told me, on the phone. The goddamn pigs."

"Please, let's not talk about it in front of the kids."

Fernand bursts out laughing. Casually, he explains, "Come on, Mom! We know all about it, you know! What, do you think we've never heard people talk about that stuff? Even Babette could teach you a thing or two …"

Bernadette smothers a laugh with her hand.

"Good God! And I wanted my children to stay innocent for as long as possible! Lord, what kind of world is this? Oh! I undertand that there isn't much respect for life these days and that girls think nothing of giving themselves over to criminal abortionists!"

"Oh, great," comments Marie-Laure, "the same old song."

"Listen, my girl, you'll soon learn that life is what matters. A society that crushes its children is damned. You're the one who's always quoting the nuns at us, 'Sister So-and-so said this, Sister So-and-so said that,' and you're contradicting me? What do those dried-up old women talk to you about? The advantages of condoms?"

"No, they don't, if you have to know. They never discuss anything vulgar. They only focus on things that are refined, things above our miserable physical existence."

"They think their farts smell like roses!" Chonchon bellows. Bored with the discussion, he moves to the table and sits down. "I'm hungry. If you kids are hungry too, come sit down. Here, Étienne, sit next to me."

"Me too," clamours Fernand, dashing forward, ready to vie for the honour.

"Of course! Fernand, you know perfectly well that I'm not going to forget about you. Fernand on his father's right, and Étienne on the left. As if we were in heaven!"

He utters a hearty, crude laugh, and pulls a flask of gin from his back pocket. He takes a few long gulps and hands the bottle to Étienne, who takes a little.

"I want some too!" demands Fernand.

"What, you? You're still wet behind the ears!"

"I want some," repeats Fernand, adding an enormous oath.

"Well, my little ruffian, if you can swear like a man, I guess you can drink like one, too. Here, but don't take it all!"

Over Lucie's weak protests, the triumphant Fernand takes the flask, laughing. He looks at her, hesitating, and brings it to his lips. The small sip instantly chokes him, and the whole table guffaws loudly. At first, Fernand laughs along with them, then his sensitivity takes over, and he turns red with fury.

"Stop laughing at me, you fuckers!"

He begins to scream, the long sustained screaming of his tantrums, beating the table with his fists, risking injury on the utensils. With a completely disgusted look, Chonchon exclaims, "Great, there he goes! Go on, take him to his room. I don't feel like listening to him scream."

He lowers his eyes before a sharp glance from Lucie.

"And you ... what's your name again?"

"Corinne."

"Oh, yes! Well, Corinne, do you like it here, with your new family?"

"Yes, sir."

"Hey, don't call me 'sir,' I'm your father. Say 'Yes, dad,' or 'Yes, Chonchon.'"

"Yes, sir — Uh, okay."

"How about you, Serge?"

An embarrassed silence greets the question.

"Do you mean 'Stéphane,' Chonchon?"

"Yes, yes. Serge, Stéphane ... Are you happy ... Goddamn it, what am I trying to ask him? ... Are you happy your sister didn't drown?"

"Dad, really!" Étienne protests.

"It's a joke!" continues Chonchon. "God, I'm exhausted. I'm not used to family reunions anymore. I'm having a hard time just being polite."

He laughs, seeking allies in the surrounding gazes and finding only confusion.

After a fairly sombre meal, with the occasional attempt at humour meeting only with solemn responses, and Chonchon, at the head of the table, playing his father's role with as much dignity as possible, Lucie, who suddenly looks very pale, says in her warm voice, "Come on, children, we're going to clean up. Chonchon, it would be really nice if you went up to see Gervais, who must be expecting you. And tell Fernand that, if he's calm, he can come back down now. Okay?"

"Right, I'm going. It'll be more fun than drying dishes."

"He hasn't improved any," mutters Marie-Laure, after he leaves the veranda.

"Give him time," says Lucie. "He's just come back. Poor man, he's not used to family life anymore."

Vincent interrupts, "Life must be pretty different with his whore. A little peck here, a little peck there ..."

"That's none of your business! That's no way to talk about your father!"

Vincent sniggers and goes back to his book. Lucie, both hands in dishwater, suddenly feels a dull pain in her right buttock. It's as if her whole body is rebelling against the tranquil horror of her life, of which she is now keenly aware. Her life hovers before her like a pile of dirty plates immersed in the soupy water, a heap of disappointments in which she recognizes her childhood dreams soiled, scarred, cracked, chipped one by one, which she cleans mechanically in readiness for further soiling, more deterioration, small omens of death. She doesn't itemize her griefs. They are there before her, in a pile, bobbing in the bitter suds. Her buttock now hurts a great deal, and she starts to shiver, she's a little dizzy. There's movement around her, and somebody grabs her, supporting her, there's a hand on her shoulder. She glimpses Étienne's sweet face, deep black eyes anxious, wondering. Everything is going dark, sinking. She's very hot, she's sinking.

20

"Looks like a diabetic coma," says one of the ambulance drivers. "We're taking her in right away. Get out of the way, you kids."

The two men run for the stretcher and load Lucie onto it, as still and white as death, with Chonchon and the children standing back watching in a circle. Oddly, no one is crying, not even little Bernadette, as if the event is too serious, or too shocking. Tears will come later, when she's no longer before their eyes, an ambiguous effigy.

"Are you going to ride with us?" the driver asks Chonchon.

"Er … no. Here, Étienne, you go. I'll stay and watch the kids. He's an adult," he adds, just in case.

"Somebody has to get her admitted. And you have to have her Medicare card."

Étienne enters Lucie's room, looks through her purse for the card, then races back outside.

The doors slam, and instantly the siren begins to emit agonizing, grotesque noises, as if the vehicle were operating in heavy traffic. Through the back window, Étienne can see his brothers and sisters clustered together, along with Chonchon, who is telling a few neighbours about what's happened.

Beside the great, recumbent form, Étienne feels a tremendous sadness. He looks at Lucie as if she's about to abandon them forever, depart to her couch of earth and shadows, sink into the oblivion of lost souls. He looks at the narrow bulging forehead, framed with greying hair, the straight nose that retains the nobility of ancient races, now lost, the mouth, sensual and pure, with its pleasant lines that seem formed solely to utter affectionate, hopeful words. Yet weariness has smeared its livid paste upon these features, and the body's slightly grotesque, misshapen mass reflects a vague defeat. Beside this prone woman, Étienne can't help but relive his afternoon's enchantment, the tender, savage possession of a sweet and wonderful body. An armful of lilies, ferns, gladioli! He pictures her breasts, upright, incredibly touching, placing his lips on them, as if on the heart of the world, the twinned star, the double God. Two breasts are a single breast, one beloved. My soul!

The ambulance reaches the hospital quickly, and the patient is dispatched to a small consulting room while Étienne goes to Admitting. He remembers coming to this place of constant bustle three years ago, accompanied by Lucie. He'd fallen off his bike and split his knee open. The wound, speckled with fine sand, took a long time to clean. Now his mother leans on him, not on Chonchon, who bowed out because he is disturbed by pain, or else indifferent to it. Probably it makes him anxious, because he'd have to rise to the occasion and might have to deal with the unexpected. Chonchon is not the man for such concerns. To Étienne, his father's cowardice — the thing that has always kept him from taking his proper place in the family — is clearer than ever.

It makes him sad, but not despondent, for now he is the man. He'll give Lucie the support she needs and he'll be there for the whole family. So far, he's only dealt with the meagre responsibilities handed to him by his mother, little concerned with delegating adulthood's duties and burdens. She loved children too much to deprive these lives entrusted to her by the Lord of the least ray of light, the slightest fragment of heaven. She took care of all the chores, while subverting them as much as she could, and handled being a mother like it was a party, continually astonished to discover how tall and large she stood among her rowdy brood. Now he will gently but firmly take over her role, the one Chonchon has evaded. He'll take charge. He'll do it for them, and for himself as well. For one day, perhaps soon, he'll have to leave, and when he does, they'll have to be able to keep going. And he will leave to start his own home, build his house. He will enter it with a woman full of grace, and they will make love there, create the world, and the wheel of days.

It's nearly ten o'clock when Étienne gets home, staggering with fatigue. He covered the three kilometres between the hospital and home on foot. When he pushes the door open, the living room is full of light, but empty. He hears voices on the veranda and goes there. Chonchon, Gervais, Vincent, and Fernand are quietly playing cards.

"Hello! And, so?" inquires Chonchon gravely.

"I didn't get to see her, but they told me that everything was going well."

"That's exactly what I thought. They didn't tell you what was wrong?"

"No. I guess she'll tell you herself tomorrow, on the phone. It seems to me that she's probably mainly really tired. The events of these last few days have upset her a lot … But there could be something else."

"The nurse was talking about diabetes …"

Conjecture drifts in the crude lamplight for a moment, then the game takes precedence once more. Gervais slams down his cards with a triumphant cry.

"And are you doing better?" asks Étienne, putting a hand on his shoulder.

"Yes, faggot."

"Why are you calling me that?"

"Because you're touching me. Get your dirty hand off me."

Disconcerted, Étienne removes his hand as the younger ones laugh maliciously.

Chonchon steps in. "Hey, you, this is none of your business. What's more, I've had enough of you. Go to bed."

"Dad!" they protest in unison, which makes them laugh even harder.

"Come on, out! Or I'll get mad."

They pretend they haven't heard him. Suddenly, Chonchon slams his fist on the table, almost knocking over the half-full bottle in front of him. The bellowed oaths and his furious manner finally convince the recalcitrants, who leave the room without a word.

Chonchon takes a long swallow, which leaves him numbed and pensive. He talks at Gervais and Étienne in a thick voice. They listen absent-mindedly, each absorbed by his own drama.

"As for me … Well, I like children just fine, but not for too long, and not too many at a time. I'm not talking about you two. You know how to shut up and think. But the younger ones … Young kids aren't always easy. Christ! … Your mother, she loves that, little kids. She wanted ten, twelve! Imagine, twelve kids! I gave her seven, and then she went and adopted two more, as if she didn't have enough problems! For her, money just doesn't matter. Poverty doesn't bother her at all. Totally destitute, for crying out loud." He laughs. "Penury is like fear. The more you have, the more it shines forth; it's like a kingdom around you, you become the king, queen of something. The queen of welfare! Look around you. It's a mess. People think the Tourangeaus are poor, but there's ten times more clothing here than in the rich people's houses. There's so much clothing that you don't know what to do with it anymore. It's piled up all over the place. What's the sense of that? You could open a business! Nice old clothes belonging to well-fed people who didn't sweat too much and didn't wear out much, beside the seat of their pants from sitting in front of the television. This, children, is affluence. We live in an affluent society and the worst thing is that the rich people have decided to smother the poor people with their affluence and dump their garbage here. Look at this! Is this a house? Of course not: it's a hole. A big hole. They put your mother in here, and you kids, and dumped a mountain of charities on you. Here, Étienne, have a little sip, it'll wake you up. You're falling asleep on me."

"No, I'm going to go to bed. I'm exhausted."

"Ah! Having a girlfriend is hard on your system, eh?" says Chonchon, with a coarse laugh.

"Him?" says Gervais. "He's nothing but a goddamn fag."

"Now, come on!" objects Chonchon. "I saw his girlfriend, and she's really pretty. And nice, too. What's her name again?"

"Good night!" Étienne tosses out as he exits quickly.

"Her name is Good Night," chuckles Chonchon. "God, this is awful!" he says, sinking back into thought. "I'm the father of seven great kids, and when I want to talk to one of them a bit, get to know him, we never get to talk for more than five minutes. Except for you, Gervais, the one who's the most like me ... Are you glad you look like me? We're exactly alike, goddamn it! We've got the same face, the same body. You know, it's been a long time since I've seen you in your birthday suit, but ..."

"For God's sake, are you like Mom? This afternoon, she was telling me, all excited, that she'd seen me naked! I'm starting to think the whole world wants to rape me, fucking Christ. I'm sick of it, sick of it!"

"There's nothing to get upset about, you poor kid! You think it's awful that those goddamned dirty bastards pushed their clubs up your ass, but when you think about it, it's not so bad. In my day, it was priests who did that. The main thing, boy, is that you didn't like it. That proves you're a man, a real man. But, when he's poor, a real man has to put up with all kinds of outrages. You have to get over it. Middle-class people are the only ones who put their honour and virtue above everything else."

He thinks for a minute, and concludes, "They're the real fags."

Gervais looks at his father. The raw light emphasizes his pale skin and brings out its alcoholic characteristics. He jumps up and runs outside, the screen door slamming behind him. Violent retching sounds reach Chonchon's ears.

"Fuck!" he thinks, completely depressed. "Another wimp. He's probably a fag and just doesn't know it."

What kind of monster was it, what kind of animal was tracking her? What did she run from with small steps, her knees full of sand, her legs like marshmallows? With her eyes now wide open, Frédérique can't remember. She was very scared, but once she emerged from the nightmare she couldn't remember the thread of it. There was only the fleeing, the heaviness. Around her, all is still. The depths of the night. Rays from the street lamp penetrate to the back of the room, and she can clearly make out Marie-Laure's outline, asleep in the next bed. When she's asleep, when she's not obsessed with doing everything right and fashioning herself after her nun teachers, Marie-Laure radiates peace and beauty, as if transfigured. She forgets even the body's constraints, the bloody napkin between her thighs, the thing that destines her for the love and contempt of men. What are her dreams, full of soft hands, smiles, warm envelopment? At least the pictures in her head contain no beasts, nothing attacks her and makes her flee with feet encased in cement. Frédérique envies her. Marie-Laure never has nightmares, her lips never pinch in a moan. She sleeps like a feather in the wind, a stick bobbing in the waves, blonde and waterlogged. The tireless rocking of the dream.

A hand on her genitals, only recently covered with thick black fleece, the other hand absentmindedly brushing already magnificent breasts, Frédérique tries to understand what is keeping her awake. There's something. It isn't Lucie's fall, her slow collapse into their arms, her face closing, depriving them all of her light. It's something else ... Oh, yes! Of course. Beside Lucie, she sees this face, this man. A repellent head, with thin gold hair, skin that is pale and red in patches, cruel features, and a gaze, an ugly gaze fastened on her. A gaze that is green like the dirty froth at water's edge that, when picked up with a stick and drained of water, turns into a thin stream of mucus. A washed-out green, bleached by alcohol and a life of ease. Yet something was kindled in that gaze, she saw a spark in those eyes when he linked her to the chimera of the past, to that Lucie, that firefly illuminating the virgin forest. In a flash, Frédérique imagines herself as her mother, a naked princess welcoming, swallowing up her young blond poet, Chonchon with his fantastic fingers and papier-mâché dreams. Because of this straying gaze ...

The crickets' grating now captures her attention and keeps her awake. Suddenly, she's unbearably hot in her thin night-gown; her back feels like it's cooking on coals. She sits up in bed, begins to take off the light garment, though her sister would be scandalized if she found her naked at dawn, then changes her mind. Better to get up, go down to the kitchen and have a glass of lemonade, maybe a snack. Nocturnal excursions like this are unusual for her, but insomnia impels her.

Barefoot, arms out to hold onto the walls in case she falls on the dark staircase, she gets to the wooden platform outside with no difficulty. She lingers there a moment, drinking in the fresh air. It must be very late, because the murmur of cars and motorcycles can no longer be heard from the highway. Only the crickets remark with mechanical liveliness on the last vestiges of heat. From the river close by she can hear the sound of a fish diving in, or a frog.

Fascinated by the mass of shadows and silence, Frédérique slowly yields to fear. She imagines menace, embodied and taking aim at her youthful, skimpily clad arrogance, her silhouette, white against the shadows. A denizen of night appears, breaks her, subdues her … One day, a man … He will rend her, force pleasure into her through every orifice, cram her, stuff her with crude delight.

She wants to feel the terror, but it doesn't come. Her wandering mind at last pulls her away from her half-formed desire; a sudden rustling of grass brings her back to reality. That's that, she's shivering, and, swiftly, she enters the house.

The veranda out back is lit up. What's going on? She walks toward it, finding Chonchon alone, asleep in his chair. What to do? Wake him up or let him sleep off all that booze? She decides to have some lemonade and a bit of cake first. Then, as she is about to leave the room, she takes pity on the man collapsed upon the table. At least she can try to lead him to bed. She gently puts her hand on the snoring, whimpering shape, gently shakes, with no result, begins again, more firmly, insisting. The man opens one eye, groaning, mumbling a few words. Frédérique thinks she can make out a name, Vanessa, his girlfriend's name. He stares at the face in front of him, his eyes focusing, filling, bit by bit, with something golden.

"Is that you?"

"I came down, I was thirsty. I saw you."

"Yes ... I fell asleep."

He lets out a big yawn, suppresses a few burps, sighs, "Goddamn booze!"

Then he pulls himself together. "But I'm not drunk, you know. I never get drunk. I'm just a bit ... Shit, a man's got to live, right? A little help ... What do you think? I don't know what you're thinking. Come, come closer. Such a pretty girl! ... That's very pretty, your nightie, very pretty, with the little flowers ... My word, you look just like a princess!"

She draws near him, simultaneously attracted and annoyed, happy to be getting some tenderness from the father she missed so much when she was little, in spite of the passionate effusions which weren't about real affection, yet repelled by the ugliness of this face, still shadowed by remnants of beauty. The Chonchon of her earliest recollection was handsome. Now he smiles, and the bit of green eye that peeps through the puffy eyelids has the soft freshness of grass. He takes her hand, sits gazing at her without a word.

"How do you manage to be so beautiful?" he murmurs. "Without any makeup, anything? Just your skin, your lips ... And your eyes, they'd tame wild beasts, they're so ... Your eyes are like the night ..."

Suddenly, Frédérique realizes that things could get bad, that this man's desire is stirring, and she feverishly casts about for a way to leave without creating a scene, stirring up trouble. A girl gives her father a kind kiss before bed. She bends her head toward him, kisses him on the forehead: "Good night, Dad. It's time to get some rest, now."

But the big man's hand has closed over hers and holds her there. He's very pale and stares at her, panting. "No, no, stay! Stay, my little girl, my silky one, we hardly know each other … If you knew how much you look like your mother, like Lucie, when I first met her! The first time, Lucie … I just about died when I saw her hair … all that black hair, an arrow straight to my heart … I saw stars … and her breasts …"

"Let … let me go. Let me go or I'll scream."

He grabs her around the waist, draws her to him. She is trembling, sobbing a little, she struggles fruitlessly, the drunkard's eyes are fixed on a point above her head, he is in the grip of something, a fury, he presses her to him and she screams, a long woman's scream that rends the night, a scream that splits life from top to bottom and wakens everything that is mired in slumber.

From the shadows, the children asleep next door call out, Bernadette begins to howl with fright. Suddenly, the front door opens, and Étienne, half-covered by his bathrobe, bursts in. He sees Chonchon and Frédérique, immobile, face to face, realizes what's going on, and, with irresistible strength, pushes his father out of the house, yelling, "Get lost, you filthy pig! Don't ever set foot here again or you'll have me to deal with!"

21

The last week has seen a lot of change at the Tourangeau house. The plan, sprouted from Étienne's brain, was quickly put into action. First, the young man paid a visit to Father Lanthier and asked for his help. With a blend of eagerness and embarrassment, the worthy priest agreed to release some parish funds. All the materials needed for repairing and repainting the house were borrowed or bought. Paint, brushes, rollers, scrapers, sandpaper, putty, and woodworking tools were quickly gathered together, and Étienne put his team to work. Without exception, all the boys and girls — even little Bernadette — were given a job to do. Ever since their eldest brother threw their infamous father out, they've been giving Étienne boundless respect and total obedience. Even the recovered Gervais seems to have placed himself under his brother's newfound authority. Only the set look in his green eyes belies the serenity of his thin smile.

And they've gotten an extraordinary assistant. If Étienne makes a fine substitute for a father who can't handle his responsibilities, Lucie, still under observation at the hospital, has found a worthy and ravishing substitute in Odile. One morning, shortly after work began, Odile showed up and took on the task of supervising the younger ones and preparing meals, very efficiently. Her beauty and sweetness made instant conquests of Étienne's siblings. Awed by such grace, Fernand and Vincent in particular are vying for the privilege of her approval. For five days now, the immense worksite has hummed with activity from dawn until well into the evening, as the blue house slowly recovers its former freshness.

They have not forgotten about the yard. Vincent and Fernand were given the job of piling the rubbish by the roadside. A city truck made a special trip, just for them. Then the boys carefully cleared the lawn of stones and cut the grass, the lawnmower a gracious loan from a neighbour. On Odile's instructions, however, they took care to skirt the prettiest clumps of wildflowers, especially the cape touch-me-nots and devil's paintbrush, whose petals toss bursts of yellow and orange from place to place.

Before the neighbours' incredulous eyes, five days of hard work have restored the property's spacious and provincial charm. They worked overtime to get it all done before Lucie comes home. She doesn't suspect a thing, though she's astonished not to have heard from Chonchon. They mumbled something unintelligible to her about him getting drunk and going back to Montreal; but all is well, thanks to Étienne, about whom his brothers and sisters sing endless praises. Ah, love! she thinks, it really changes a man. Love! Her boy, her big boy is in love!

She hasn't met Odile, but feels like she's an ally. She pictures her as charming, strong, with that healthy adoration for children that she has herself — in fact, a true woman, devoted to life, obstinately tender and affectionate.

Weakened by the long rest and anxious, too, knowing

that the illness that now inhabits her must be treated with respect, with caution and medication, day by day, Lucie lets Étienne take her home. He has called a taxi. Her grown son has an odd air about him under his sunny sweetness — as if he's hiding something.

On the way home, the taxi drives through the neighbourhood where Dr. Tourangeau had lived with his descendants. Their old house is now city property, and seeing it turned into an office building strikes Lucie through the heart. She will now never be able to return to this corner of the past for which she has so much affection. For her, in spite of all the setbacks, it is synonymous with happiness, in particular, those seven pregnancies, which have turned out so well, and affection from a father-in-law whose heart was as big as the world.

Musing on the irrevocable changes wrought by destiny somewhat overshadows the rest of the trip, though she feels an intensifying eagerness about being back with her brood. She's seen them just once, during visiting hours, in her hospital room's efficient and gloomy atmosphere.

"Mom," says Étienne, with poorly masked impatience, as the taxi turns onto the street that runs along the water, "Close your eyes now. I'll tell you when you can open them."

It's beautiful, really beautiful, really. That's it. They've fixed everything up, the house, the yard. Nest and branch. They pulled together, worked very hard, led by the little master and his lady, and turned the house upside down. They're like servants, awaiting the homecoming of Mistress Lah-di-dah.

They're handsome, well fed, clean. That girl, young woman, that's Odile. She is modest and triumphant, just as it should be. A beauty, too, the naturally distinguished kind, full of charm. Exactly Étienne's type; he couldn't resist her. And good, too. She has done her good deed and Fernand is pleased as punch beside her. I'm wiping away a tear. Yes, Étienne, it's beautiful, yes, I'm happy. I can't get over it, you've done so much. You shouldn't have. You're spoiling me. I'm not saying much, my mouth seems to be frozen, but it's the surprise of it all. The surprise is killing me. My arms are paralyzed, can't you see? It wouldn't take much to make me faint, like the other day when the pain rose from my buttocks to my head. But today I'm going to resist it. The ambulance, the hospital, they're expensive. I'm going to concentrate on turning my surprise into joy and figuring out what I owe you. How you love me! You make me so happy! It seems like a real middle-class house, a white man's lawn, charming, but you've kept little wild nooks for your mother the squaw, who loves crazy flowers. Devil's paintbrush. You've worked like slaves, patching everything up, repainting, it's like new. I'll bet that inside the walls are sparkling again, and it's all tidy — what did you do with it all? What did you do with the clothes, the piles and piles of clothing, and the dirty dishes, and the garbage, and Chonchon? Come, come here, children, let me hug you, my eyes full of tears, my voice breaking, and you first, Étienne, handsome leader, looking at me like you're worried I won't fully appreciate all your devotion, you big silly, and here is the auburn Odile, pretty tresses framing her cheeks, her beautiful face, so good and sweet, a sumptuous, self-conscious body that I can clearly picture being given to pleasure, you filthy thing pumping the substance out of my foolish son, forever taken from me, from his childhood, his happiness. And you, come here, my big girls and boys full of childhood's lovely sins, and you too, Corinne and Stéphane, for me no different from the others, you're my children just as much they are, and Étienne's, as well, since he is now our master, our reigning lord. This is a big day, I'm back with you, and now I won't weigh on your destinies any longer because you've found your way, an honourable way. Now we're honourable, I never expected that. Anything but that. I'm so weak. I'm going to have to learn how to live, how to live here. Without getting anything dirty. I'll have proper relationships with my children, my neighbours, my son and his vixen — forgive me! I'll be happy every day, and I'll set a good example. No more midnight lovers, dopes and bastards, pigs and priests. My bed will be spotless, too, I'll be a saint. That's it, the new masters could have my room, and I'll sleep somewhere else, like the living room, the laundry room. What, Vincent? You want to know how I like it? Well, it's wonderful! You're all darlings. And you, Marie-Laure, you want to know if I missed you? Oh, yes! my girl, much more than you missed me. You didn't have much time to think about your poor sick mother, your damn messy crazy slut of a mother. Ah! the joy of reunions! I'm crying hard now, now I'm feeling it. Is this what you were waiting for? It took some time, but here it is. I'm making up for it, I'm opening my trap. It's a cloudburst, blessed deluge! It feels so good to cry!

22

The night spent in the cozy comfort of her girlhood bed, Odile, still half-asleep, goes into the kitchen, a thin dressing gown carelessly buttoned around her. The sun is already high. She heads for the automatic coffee maker and pours the rest of the black, aromatic liquid into her cup. She puts in milk, a little sugar, and sits down at the table. Nine-thirty! A good girl's remorse pierces through her indolence. She, who always rises at seven, ready to embark on her program of scales and exercises or, during the school year, glean the knowledge that will one day make her a competent, dynamic career woman! A career woman … Today, for some reason the words repel her. She glimpses a lifetime hedged about by duty and rules, driven by a horrid imperative to succeed. Now, something inside her combats the old dream that matches the hopes her parents cherish for her, her father in particular.

She isn't completely rejecting what she's valued all these years, but love has shown her something different, as if she has suddenly glimpsed a whole other part of life — the most important part. Doubtless she can reconcile it with the reasoned principles that have guided her life so far. Why would it be otherwise? There are lots of people, her parents for example, who've been able to handle the practical side of career and

family while satisfying deeper needs, more personal, private …
Though, Odile wonders, astounded that she's never thought
about it before, do Mom and Dad really love each other
romantically, the way I love Étienne, and Étienne loves me?
Have they ever felt that grand passion, the passion that
enflames the body and instantly changes how you see things,
the way you think? Her father's face rises to mind. It's an
authoritarian face that seems eroded by a profound disen-
chantment. The eyes contain little of the joy that makes living easy. Sometimes, when he looks at her, his daughter, a kind
of flash dissipates the haze of bitterness, but that's because he's
thinking about the honours she will reap for him in spite of her
femaleness. To succeed like a man: that's the goal Odile has
always aimed for, without really being aware of it, simply com-
plying with the family's designs. Music alone has been a clear
space amongst the constant hours of work and ambition.

Love has now shown her that she is also body and spirit,
and that men — thank God — are not all cut from her father's
cloth. Suddenly, she suspects that he's deeply unhappy. What
other reason could there be for his propensity for constant
grumbling and condemning the slightest divergence from his
strict ideas of order and honour?

Her father. In truth, no, he couldn't possibly be unhappy,
this cold man who is bereft of imagination. He only cares about
professional success and constantly adding to his wealth. With
his wife, he is correct but unaffectionate. Odile, from certain
signs she recollects but never paid attention to before, guesses
what sacrifices her mother has made to earn her reputation as a
model wife. Unexplained absences by the lord and master, her

mother's tears, poorly contained after a clearly sleepless night, enable the girl to put together a long chronicle of infidelity that, until now, has seemed like a fantasy, like the dream images from which awareness turns as soon as it leaves night behind for day. It's not really a discovery. Odile knows only that, until now, out of respect for propriety, she has refused to think about it. Her mother herself discouraged any show of sympathy from her. Grown-ups have their own inscrutable and private rituals, and the guidelines Odile has followed meant pretending nothing was wrong, while believing as hard as she could in the goodness of God and the integrity of those He placed around her. Every Sunday, the Louviers attended mass, the very model of the right-thinking and united family. God rewarded the lawyer's merits with material goods, a virtuous spouse, and children who honoured him by following in his footsteps — with success, in fact! Difficult to see how it could be greater. This man cheated on his wife, who strove to gently suppress her suffering and mould her heart and body to her fate as a professional's wife. God sanctioned the sacrifice.

Odile can't believe she's lived with a lie for so long, a lie that is at one with security, with the enormous residence that is penetrated by birdsong, the rustling of leaves, the ripening summer's perfume, the shouts of a few children playing proper games. It's such a peaceful neighbourhood! There are only opulent properties here; it's the culmination of an entire people's good taste, a happy blend of Victorian and New England styles. Here, people can suffer and die in silence, dignity. Women like Odile's mother, manicured from hair to toes, tend their gentle distress in a golden prison. They have received life sentences from tyrannical husbands, whom they worship more intensely as his absences grow more frequent, absences entailed by unfathomable duties. Odile casts a critical eye over the bright kitchen, its restrained luxury; it has no specific style, yet everything fosters superficial connections with people, and with things. The veranda at Devil's Paintbrush — that's the name she and Étienne have given the blue house in its new skin — suddenly comes to mind. Its windows open over the river's shaded bank, and nature washes in. She instantly sees the children's bright smiles, little Bernadette especially, who was so willing and patient in carrying out the tedious jobs. In this little one, a housekeeper's instincts seemed to be blooming spontaneously; until now, she had been barred from chores. She'd been touched by Bernadette's brothers, too, Vincent and Fernand; there, she'd sensed the dawning of the competitive spirit that a feminine presence can inspire in two budding males. They have such vitality, this family in which she saw such strong echoes of the young man, so calm and powerful, with whom she was more and more in love each day. From them she had also created a picture of the mother, Lucie, before she met her. She imagined much honesty and, under her chaotic side, solid common sense intent on affirming life's strengths. When at last she saw the large woman, pale and thin after her stay in the hospital, she had not been at all disappointed, but, through the transports of homecoming, she thought she'd felt a hidden reticence, even disapproval, very unlike the allegiance she'd hoped for. Lucie's big, brown, good eyes, so easily imbued with friendliness, had trouble hiding a glint of coldness. It had struck Odile; doubtless she'd expected her hero's mother to return her trust and affection in full.

Odile has reached this point in her reflections when Mrs. Louvier, as neat as a new pin, as if it were five o'clock, suddenly invests the kitchen with her energetic good taste. The woman busies herself from dawn to dusk at an infinite number of small tasks that require only a judicious intervention, a touch given to this arrangement of objects, or that balance in relationships. Upon seeing Odile, still clad in her pajamas, she feigns astonishment.

"Well! Here's a girl who has fallen victim to the demon of laziness!"

Odile smiles, stretches a little, and confesses, "Yes, once in a while, it's really nice to do *nothing*!"

"What's this? Is that my daughter, uttering those horribly normal words!"

"Normal, yes, but still outrageous, right? Mom, you are as busy as a bee from morning to night. You never waste a minute of your time. Have you ever been able to just stroll around and watch life go by?"

"Actually, no. It's much more interesting to take care of my little duties than indulge in useless daydreams, which lead nowhere, anyway. You're a lot like me in that. But what about your piano? Since your last lesson, your enthusiasm seems to have dropped off a great deal."

"That could be, Mom ... Well, my goodness, I can certainly tell you what you've probably already guessed, right?"

"What, have you fallen in love?" she teases.

Instead of an answer, Odile smiles broadly. Taken by surprise, her mother doesn't know what to say.

"Really? You …"

"Yes, Mom. I've met somebody …"

She wants to utter the miracle, call up, describe the tall boy with dark eyes, hair as black as night, features as open as lightning, yet softer than a chickadee's plump head. But these are private things, the things that create the necessary selfishness of first love.

"My dear Odile! Do you mean to tell me that you're really in love?"

"Yes, Mom. His name is Étienne."

"Étienne? That's a nice name."

Mrs. Louvier sits down, astounded at the news and even more astonished at her daughter's confidences, since mother and daughter rarely talk about anything personal. Suddenly, she's afraid of being caught off guard and learning something she'd rather know nothing about.

"Do we, do your father and I know his parents?"

"No, I doubt it. The Tourangeaus live in Two Mountains."

"So is that where you were every day last week? You told me that you were helping friends with some work."

"It was at his house. He lives with his mother and his little brothers and sisters, and they decided to paint the whole house. It's a big house by the water."

"With his mother, you said? Is his father dead?"

"No … his parents are separated."

"Ah!"

"His father is a well-known artist — you know, Chonchon, the one who makes the plush toys."

"That rings a bell."

"You gave me one once. It was that little old woman with several noses, tentacles …"

"Yes, yes, I remember. They were called 'chimeras.' Everybody wanted one."

"I visited his studio with Étienne. It was incredible!"

"Well! Maybe you shouldn't say anything to your father. I don't know how happy he'd be with you hanging out with 'artists.' He already has enough trouble with all the hours you spend practising the piano."

"It's a perfectly respectable neighbourhood. And, you know, Étienne, he's not only very handsome and smart, but he's also generous, sensitive, devoted. No one I know is as good as he is. Yes, he's good. I never thought I would ever meet someone so wonderful."

Berthe Louvier does not know how to react to this piece of news, worried by the unfamiliar fringes. She opts for smiling benevolently, and formulates her reservations carefully. "Forgive me for saying so, but I can see he's really gotten to you, Odile. I hope you're not getting carried away. You know, these infatuations sometimes have a high price."

"Come on, Mom! If you knew how happy I am! It's the first time! And it'll be the only time, I'm sure of it!"

Mrs. Louvier bursts into laughter, disarmed by such simplicity. "My dear Odile! You're head over heels, I can see that! I hope with all my heart that you'll be really happy. You deserve it. But, you know, that doesn't always happen the first time. In fact, it's pretty rare, and true love, lasting love, doesn't always begin at first sight. Your father and I …"

"Yes, how was it with you and dad? You've never really talked to me about it."

"Well, it started very slowly, you know. I … I loved someone, a young man. He was quite poor, and your grandparents were worried I would marry him. Of course I couldn't understand why they were against it. I was really unhappy for a few months. I was torn between this … adolescent … love, and wanting to respect my parents' opinion. And then, one day, your father, who attended our church, started to court me, and little by little …"

"What! You gave up the love of your life for security? You married a man you didn't love just to please your parents?"

"Of course not! You've got it all backwards. I loved your father, of course! I just mean that, when you get married, it's for a long time, and you have to be wise, give yourself every chance at happiness. It takes a lot of money to raise a family, educate your children properly, all that!"

Odile does not reply to these words of reason. They disappoint her, striving as they do to cut everything down to size, mercilessly put out the fires of passion. Maybe she shouldn't have confided in her. Yet she would have had to tell her parents about it sooner or later. Now her mother will handle the rest of the job and break the news to her father.

"Will we have the pleasure of meeting this marvellous young man?" asks Mrs. Louvier, carefully cheerful. "Maybe you could invite him to the house one day this week."

Delighted at this sudden opening, in spite of the hazy risks it presents, Odile jumps for joy and hugs her mother, lavishing her with thanks.

23

As he walks by the church, Étienne feels a need to stop in, to thank the great, good, holy Lord for all the good things He has showered on him since that fateful encounter. The young man has not entered this place for many years, except on very rare special occasions — it is frequented only by schoolchildren and the elderly. Extensive boredom is what he primarily remembers from his childhood devotions. Today, though, he wants to kneel, gaze at the high altar with its gilded tiers, and imagine a God of flesh and bone, or tarnished brass, a God whom he will thank, simply, the way one thanks a man. It is the priest who will have to be thanked for everything else, for all his generosity to the Tourangeau family. But Étienne has felt a little embarrassed about him ever since Fernand, in a gale of laughter, told him some dubious things about the cleric's call upon Lucie a while ago. A revelation delayed since Fernand had utterly forgotten to tell his siblings about the results of his spying, distracted by the events that followed, and particularly by his father's arrival. In fact, he'd risked a peep through Lucie's window and seen some odd antics. Étienne now understands the priest's somewhat embarrassed open-handedness and wonders whether it would be better to let him stew in his depravity in peace. He also knows why his mother then seemed so unconcerned about their strict benefactor. She really had him, she'd said. This kind of tactic was fair enough when your only weapon in life is your body, the poor man's only property. Poverty, which has no options, doesn't quibble over the nature of its expedients.

The door's golden handle doesn't budge, in league with the inertia of the walls, the ponderous stone façade whose silent allegories of glass and bronze jut out over Étienne's head. The church is rarely open during the week — Étienne should have remembered that. Except during rare services, God isn't there for anyone.

Entangled in futile gratitude, he's about to be on his way, but the need to say something to Father Lanthier returns, stronger than ever. His heart overflows with gratitude now that he's in love and the future is bright with meaning. The priest could also give him some advice on what to study. Behind the man of flesh — whose weaknesses Étienne is well placed to understand now that he has tasted the extraordinary pleasures of love's commerce — there is God's representative on this earth, and Étienne wants to believe in God, in the One who makes the miracle of chance encounters possible.

He nimbly skirts the presbytery's steps and presses the bell, whose muffled tones echo back to him. A little nervous, he waits before the glass-paned door with its inconsequential lacy screen. The varnished wood is the colour of sponge toffee, and he keeps his eyes focused on it, not wanting to be indiscreet. A shadow, capped in white, soon materializes behind the glass. The housekeeper opens the door.

"Excuse me, ma'am ... Miss ... could I please see Father Lanthier?"

"Come back during office hours. The Father is busy."

"I'm sorry ... What are the office hours?"

"Can't you read? They're right there, in black and white."

There's a little sign. It had been right before his eyes, but he hadn't noticed it. "I wasn't paying attention. I'm sorry I bothered you."

He turns away, but the housekeeper, impressed by his politeness and pleasant air, calls him back.

"You're one of the Tourangeau kids, aren't you? You were here not long ago to see Father Lanthier."

"Yes. It must have been during office hours. I didn't know he wasn't available at other times."

"Don't worry about it, it doesn't matter. So what happened? Did you give your mother a lovely surprise?"

Astonished, Étienne examines the unattractive face that opens remarkably intense grey-green eyes at him, revealing an utter innocence.

"Ah! You know about that."

"Yes. Father Lanthier told me. He said you wanted to fix everything up."

"Well ... yes, we did. We worked really hard, and I just wanted to let Father Lanthier know, and thank him."

"Come in, then. I'll go get him."

"Don't disturb him, I'll come by some other time."

"No, no! It'll make the poor man really happy! The people he helps don't often think of showing him how grateful they are. Wait here, it won't be long."

Étienne lets himself be shown into a small parlour, and the gossip vanishes promptly.

Sombrely furnished, the room's only decoration is a lithograph of Christ. The divine Saviour's feminine fingers point limply to his flaming heart. Further away, daylight enters through a large window. The window overlooks the small river that bisects the town, its banks shaded by ancient ash trees. Étienne is absorbed by the view of nature, pleasant, almost grand, unspoiled by the few modest old cottages. Then he pictures himself, ten days earlier, in the room next door that serves as an office. He'd been so intimidated, so anxious to achieve his goal that he hadn't paid attention to his surroundings. Only the priest's face had struck him. It almost seemed like he was making an effort to appear dignified, but his mind was wandering and he kept blushing. Keeping his dignity had not been easy, in fact. How would he be today? Étienne really has to hide the fact that he knows.

The sound of a firm footstep brings his wait to an end. Clad in dark colours, the priest appears at the door, holding out his hand to his young guest.

"So it's you. Marthe, my housekeeper, didn't want to tell me who it was. She's somewhat eccentric. She loves to surprise me!"

"I didn't mean to interrupt you. I didn't know what the office hours were."

"You're not interrupting. So, what can I do for you?"

"Actually, nothing, Father. I just dropped by to tell you how grateful I am. Thanks to you, the house has been patched up from top to bottom. It's just like new! And the whole yard is clean now."

"Good, good! That is excellent news, my dear Étienne. I'll have to go see it, one of these days. Well … if there's room in my schedule. And your mother, is she home yet?"

"Yes, she was released from the hospital a few days ago."

"She must have been very surprised!"

"Yes …"

Étienne suddenly looks worried. He hesitates, then decides to say what's on his mind. "Yes, but I'm not sure if she really liked the surprise. I expected her to be more enthusiastic."

"Bah! Perhaps being sick kept her from being more responsive. Such a sudden, major change could have … how should I say this … put her off."

"Maybe. I'm worried there might be something else, but I don't know what. But my brothers and sisters are very proud of what they've accomplished. Everybody helped. Now, whenever anybody makes a mess or gets something dirty, the others are on his back. I don't know if it will last, but, for now, our house is one of the most beautiful on the river!"

"And what a magnificent location!" adds the priest. "It has a superb view."

"This place you got us is really wonderful, Father. Now I'm old enough to realize how much we owe you, and I promise you that in the future the Tourangeau family will be worthy of your trust."

Étienne holds his hand out, and the priest, moved, takes it, mumbling, "Well … You're a good young man, Étienne … You know, people say things … about you, about your family. Your mother … Well, she has her own way of doing things, but she has a heart of gold, a really kind heart, you know that just as well as I do. And your father, too … a true artist! I knew him well, Chonchon, when he was a choir boy — I was a young vicar, and I always found him delightful, in spite of … Well, he had his faults. But he was always looking, looking for something that other people don't strive after. A kind of dream … Yes, that's it: a chimera. Chimera!"

"He's still looking for it," says Étienne, smiling.

"Is it true, what I've been told, that you had a fight with him?"

Face clouded, Étienne replies, seriously, "Father, there are things that just cannot be tolerated in a house where some principles are still respected. I can't tell you any more."

"Well … Yes, I suppose you're right. It's too bad that modern life makes things so hard for so many people. All these broken families, separated, even divorced couples! And religion, almost everyone has abandoned it! It seems to me that, in the old days, there was more happiness to go around, don't you think?"

"I don't know, Father. Things have always been kind of chaotic at my house, even though, as you were saying earlier, Mom has a heart of gold and has taught us how to love. Love ourselves, first of all, and love each other. But now, Father, I'm an adult, I want to lead a good life, a proper life, and I want my family to do better too, like me. That's why I took on the work with which you helped us so much, and I want you to know that I'm not going to show you my gratitude only with words, but by taking care of my responsibilities, as the oldest son, and, well, the head of the family."

These solemn words come easily to Étienne. Ever since he fell in love, every succeeding day has shown him more and more that he has an adult's resources.

"Étienne, with all my heart, I hope you succeed. You are a man, truly, and I will pray for God to help you. Courageous young people like you are rare. But, tell me, what are your plans for the future, practically speaking?"

"First, Father, I want to go back to school and finish Cegep. That way, next year I can start university. But I have to find a job. I'm a bit worried about it because it's really hard to find a good job that still leaves time for school. But I'm determined to work really hard. I have to achieve my goals. My happiness depends on it …"

In the glow that lights Étienne's eyes, the priest glimpses something beyond a poor boy's ambition, a determination to climb out of poverty — perhaps the profound conviction that a very powerful emotion sometimes kindles in kindly hearts, making them strong against the world's unsettling challenge.

24

Before he goes in, Étienne pauses a moment before the big house that, for him, illuminates the bright name bestowed upon it by Odile, Devil's Paintbrush. With the recent rains, the yard has become evenly green once more; here and there, clumps of wildflowers brandish their bouquets of light. Now the property has nothing to envy its neighbours, which often appear showy and pretentious, less well suited to the placid setting of water and greenery. Beyond the lot, the river's broad back bears a cloud-filled sky, submitting to its slow, synchronous gyrations. Under its light-filled surface, Étienne can't help thinking about the abyss. Lucie, who'd consulted a survey map, had often talked about it, quoting neighbours who'd complacently listed the rubbish that shore dwellers had consigned to the shadows of its depths. Then his thoughts drift to the rapids, which he can't see from here, and the islands near the train bridge. It is there, among the trunks of great trees, among the warm whispers of water and wind-dried shrubbery, that he'd held the world's bright beauty in his arms, beneath his body, irrevocably penetrated that tender nest. There, in a single moment, his life took root, fixing the burden of emotion that had been building in his heart from the time they'd first seen each other, from the first innocent, sweet words they'd uttered, seated side by side on the

small commuter train. From the abyss to the island, the island
to the railroad tracks, Étienne goes upstream, to where his life
as a man began, where, in a flash, he became strong in the face
of death. Strong in the face of his mother, too, the large, good,
crazy woman who, without knowing or wishing it, bewitches
her children, keeps them prisoner in an almost inviolable circle. Beyond this circle, there is the charming, unhoped-for
princess, her face sculpted by the flame of kisses, and it is she
that Étienne bears in his heart, now and forever, like a perpetual star from whom all light comes.

As he opens the door, Étienne is halted by the sight of a
mound of clothes between the armchairs. The main room —
in which Fernand and Vincent are busy taking apart the television — is in a considerable mess.

"What's going on here?" he exclaims, stunned and angry.

"The goddamn TV hasn't worked for a month, and you
know it," Vincent answers. "Since nobody seems to be in a big
hurry to get it fixed, I want to try and see what's wrong with it."

"But you don't know anything about it! Those things are
dangerous, they can blow up if you play around with them. I
know you: all you're going to do is take it apart and leave
everything all over the place."

"So?" says Fernand, aggressively. "What's wrong with that?
Who's it going to hurt if things are a bit messy? What do you
think we are, maids?"

He laughs, a cutting, idiotic cackle.

"And where did all these clothes come from?"

"They're from Mrs. Pomerleau, you know, lady bountiful.
She brought them over a little while ago."

"But I asked people to stop dumping those rags on us."

"She phoned before she came over," Vincent explains. "She talked to Mom."

Highly annoyed, Étienne heads to the kitchen, followed by the poorly contained laughter of his two brothers.

"Mom?"

Near the table, Marie-Laure is combing out her long russet hair, which she has just washed. She wears a pale green dressing gown and each motion of her raised arms parts her gown, revealing small pointed breasts dotted with a few freckles. Étienne, embarrassed, averts his eyes, asking, "Where's Mom?"

"In her room. She's tired, so she went back to bed."

"At eleven o'clock in the morning! What do you think, Marie-Laure? Is she as sick as all that?"

"Sick? I don't know. She's tired, anyway," she says, lowering her voice so she can't be heard from her mother's room. "Since she came back, I've had the impression that something's bothering her, as if she doesn't care about us anymore! It seems like her family just doesn't matter to her. Maybe she's depressed. That's pretty common when you've been really sick. All the pampering she did to make Stéphane and Corinne forget what they went through, and now she barely talks to them. Fernand's the only one who can get a smile out of her, with his weird ideas. You know, I think that one's really dangerous. If he can't control himself better than that, I don't know what he'll become!"

"Yet he's been behaving himself these last two weeks."

"Don't kid yourself. I get the feeling he's working up to one of his tantrums!"

"Good Grief! Is it going to start all over again? When I came in earlier, it was obvious that we're sliding back into our untidy ways. The main room is a disaster."

"Bah! You can't change a family's habits just like that. And, well, maybe it's better like that."

"What are you saying!"

Marie-Laure turns her beautiful, clear-eyed, cynical gaze on him. In that robe, with her head emerging above it like fine porcelain, she looks like an angel of bitter reason — the kind of reason that gets one through the wreck of hopes.

"There are some changes that just aren't worth the trouble. Mediocrity is often better than some luxuries, no matter how seductive they are."

"What do you mean?"

"Just that. When you start off life in the dirt …"

"Christ! You really have to like dirt to want to stay in it."

"Étienne!"

The weakened voice comes from the closed room. Étienne opens the door a crack and asks, in a low voice, "Mom, did you call me?"

"Come here, love, I have to talk to you. Close the door behind you. I just want to talk to you alone, my grown-up boy."

"You're not too tired? How are you feeling today?"

The recumbent, slightly shrunken form, whose thinness pains him, reminds Étienne of the trip to the hospital when, in the ambulance, for the first time his mother suddenly stopped being a beneficent giant, the pillar the whole family clung to, to fend off disaster. Wrapped like a mummy in the stretcher's bedding, she was once more the child she had always been at heart, an overly large child encumbered by her body and her duties. Now, in the bed that smells like too much sleep, her head and the top of her chest emerge from the wrinkled sheet like a dull apparition.

"Come, sit here on the edge of the bed, the way you used to, not so long ago, do you remember? We used to have long talks; you'd tell me everything that was on your mind, especially after your dad left."

"And you used to tickle me, and I didn't like that," he growls, smiling.

"I tickled you? Come on, a mother doesn't do that kind of thing!"

"Well, I said I didn't like it, but it made the bobos go away and it made me feel better inside."

"What can I say, love? I was crazy! I've always liked to play. When I was little, I didn't have anyone to play with. No one. Only my old dad, but he …"

"I know."

"No, you don't know. But it doesn't matter. You matter, you and the rest of them. The past isn't important. Tell me what's going on with you. Talk to me about … her."

As she speaks these last words, her face gets paler still. To Étienne, her lips seem like slashes in her face, dried by fever.

"Odile …"

He collects himself, looking for the right words, words that won't diminish Lucie's good will, for he sees how hard it is for her to accept the woman who has come into his life and he doesn't understand why. Isn't Odile good, as she is, and beautiful, and capable of loving unreservedly?

"It seems like, since I met her, nothing is the same. It's as if something's gripping me inside, like I could start laughing or crying at any time. It's really upsetting, because I feel like it can't be true, that my happiness is going to disappear, abandon me, like … like a child who's lost his mother. And, at the same time, I can't get over it, the fact that she chose me, loves me. I've held her, Mom. I've held her in my hands, in my arms, and she's mine, all mine, Mom, gives herself to me wholeheartedly, her whole body, and I'm me, at last, I'm myself, a man, do you understand? I finally understand what I am, what I have, why I have a penis. I have a penis for her, Mom, through her, it makes us one, one whole, we are a blossom pulsing at the centre, radiating its joy, its affection everywhere, and its power, too. Love makes us powerful, Mom, it kills us, and gives birth to us!"

She gazes at him, stunned, and two tears slide down her nose and around her lips. "What you're saying is lovely, Étienne. You're very handsome, son, and I can see why the girls go for you. You remember the day you met her? That morning, before you left, I talked to you about girls, and you said to me, you silly fool, that they weren't interested in you, and you'd be better off if you were a fag. Fag!"

They laugh. Then Étienne explains, "That's before I knew Odile. She isn't like the others. She doesn't want a guy to take her to the movies, out for dinner, who'll dazzle her with a big car and promise her the good life."

"Yes, I know."

Étienne doesn't like this laconic answer, which once again shows how much opposition Lucie is secretly putting up to his happiness. He questions her, in a voice tinged with impatience, "I've got the feeling, Mom, that you blame Odile for something, and I'd like to know what!"

She is quiet for a long time, seeming to search around, as if she wanted to pull threads together, threads from an infinitely delicate weave that only make sense when completely joined. Then she begins to speak, softly at first, then with a voice that is increasingly urgent and desolate, as if powerless to stave off the horrors of fate.

"Yes, Odile is very nice, my dear Étienne. She seems like a princess ... not an Indian princess from the forest, but a princess like in the old stories, beautiful, sweet, and good, too, who can deal with life, although all her courtiers keep bad things away from her. Yes, I'm very happy for you, happy, but ... What can I say? How can I make you understand? Your Odile has parents, she has a house, a background ... It's very different from what you're used to! When I came back from the hospital, and saw the house all repainted, tidy, cleaner than it has ever been, I knew right away ... I knew that she would never be able to live the way we do, and you'd want to make us over, reform us, make us worthy of her, and the worst part, Étienne, is that you're right! I'm a pig, I'm crazy, I know it's true. I've often been made to feel that way, and people have even yelled that at me! That fat Garon came here to insult me, threaten me. The rest, the mayor, the city councillors, the town leaders, they all agree with him. Those people have no mercy on people who won't live the way they do, especially when there's Indian blood in their veins. I'm half Mohawk, and proud of it, but in their eyes, I'm almost a witch, even though I'm pro-life and I fight against abortion. They don't lose sleep about life, but a big family that has a hard time making ends meet and doesn't live in the lap of luxury, that bothers them because they want everybody to be just like them. And your Odile, son, even if she's nice and smart and generous, she's still from that world, she grew up in comfortable, refined surroundings, she studied piano, went to a good school, and, in the fall, she's starting law school. That's good, that's wonderful, but do you think she can be happy with what you can give her? And even if the love you have for each other can get past that obstacle, erase the fact that you have unequal backgrounds, do you think her parents are going to let her walk off with a Tourangeau kid? She may be an adult, but maybe she's not ready to leave her past behind her so she can live with the man she loves. Did you think about that?"

"But Mom, I'm determined to do everything I can to succeed. I'm going to finish Cegep, and go to university, too ..."

"Is that right? And how long will all that take, until you get your degree? And, once you've got it, do you think it's going to be easy to get a job? It seems to me that just last year you were begging me to let you drop out of school, so just what is it that you want to be, all of a sudden? A doctor? A lawyer?"

"Uh ... I thought ... An oceanographer ..."

Lucie is taken by surprise, and her eyes open wide. "What? What are you talking about! Did you say oceanographer? What do oceanographers live on during the winter?"

She laughs out loud as Étienne, humiliated, tries to explain: "I saw a show on television about it ... I thought to myself that that is what I wanted to be, if I went to university. An oceanographer studies ocean currents, tides, the dynamics of water."

"Well! If you manage to do it, and Chonchon finds out, he'd burst with pride to have an oceanographer for a son! By all the saints! It probably takes years and years to become an oceanographer, and what are you and Odile going to do in the meantime? Do you want to live together? Things aren't easy, you know, with this recession. You can't live on air. And are you sure you'll be going to school in the same city? Can you take that kind of specialized program here in Montreal?"

"I don't know, Mom, we'll see when we get there. One step at a time. First I have to finish Cegep, and to do that, I have to get a job — part-time, of course."

"Oh, here we go again. You have such a hard head! Haven't I told you a thousand times that I could lose my income if they found out you're earning money?"

This time, though, Étienne has talked to Odile, who knows more about it, and he rebels. He threatens to phone Social Services then and there to find out exactly what the law says. Lucie immediately beats a retreat, and he suddenly realizes how she has kept the wool pulled over his eyes with silly lies, and for how long, just to keep him close to her. She's a drain, a real whirlpool, this overgrown child who can't contemplate the solitude of a mother whose job is done, so greedy for the lives she has released into the world that she can't cut the umbilical cord! Étienne contemplates her, thin yet huge under the sheet, looks at her earth-coloured skin, her tousled hair, her still-beautiful face now beginning to show the shadows of decline. He'd swear at her, beat her, but that the unreason of her mother's love makes her pathetic, massed in an atmosphere darkened by her lies and folly.

25

"You met on the train?"

Mrs. Louvier asks the question in an even voice that is as impenetrable as her face. Étienne is sitting, very straight, in an armchair. Odile, on the sofa, swings her leg nervously. As a respectful and responsible daughter, she had a duty to introduce her lover to her parents, but now she's very worried that she'll run into an insurmountable wall of prejudice. Her father, with his abrupt manners, is particularly likely to raise the tension level. Thank goodness he's not home from work yet.

"Yes," Étienne replies, with a bit of confidence. "The train was packed, and there was an empty seat beside me. So it was just by accident that ..."

"That's right," Odile confirms. "Chance did everything right, that day."

A little wrinkle in the surface of the conversation, a gentle laugh. Bathed in the living room's blue and amber light, the eclectic furniture attests to expensive elegance. The thick carpet with its cream tints is Oriental. Étienne's foot partly covers a blue and pink flower that looks a lot like a dragon's mouth, and he moves it, as if he were crushing a real flower. Here, everything lives, but silently, and there are traps everywhere. He feels like he's being tested. Odile had warned him what to expect, but asked him to go along with the ritual with a good grace. "It doesn't matter what they think," she'd told him. "I'm an adult, and they can't keep me from living my life as I see fit. Do it because you love me." And, for love, because of his immense love, he's there, sitting in an armchair that's too soft, unable to relax, watching that perfect woman come and go, still young, wearing a bit too much eye makeup, busying herself at trivial, useless tasks so that she won't have to sit down anywhere and have a real conversation.

"Are you at law school?"

"No. I still have a year of Cegep left."

"Ah!"

"And I don't plan to be a lawyer."

"What are your plans, then?"

"If possible, I'd really like to study oceanography."

"How interesting! But don't you have to leave Montreal for that?"

"I haven't looked into it yet. I'm going to do it over the next few months. Of course, I have to finish Cegep first."

"True! Are you younger than Odile, by any chance?"

"No ... I had to drop out of school for a year."

"Are you in poor health?"

"Uh ... yes, that's it." Caught off guard, Étienne catches himself in a pathetic lie, and he's furious with himself, more so because Odile is there watching him flounder. But it would be too complicated to explain his meandering academic career to this perfect lady who is nothing like the wonderful girl she brought into the world. He's greatly relieved, as is Odile, whose reactions he is watching out of the corner of his eye, when Mrs. Louvier drops the subject, suddenly exclaiming: "Oh! Odile, didn't you tell me that Mr. … Tourangeau, right? — May I call you Étienne? Let's not stand on ceremony! — What was I saying? Oh, yes! Didn't you say that Étienne wanted to hear you play the piano? That's right, you've never had a chance to enjoy our little musician's talent, have you? I'm going to leave you because I have to make dinner, and I've been hearing those beautiful pieces for a long time now!"

"I never know," says Odile, after she leaves, "whether to bless her for her tact and understanding or be mad at her for her hidden agenda."

"She's very nice," says Étienne, without much conviction.

"And you," says Odile, laughing, "are a tremendous liar. I didn't know you could be so bourgeois!"

"My grandfather helped to bring me up, a little. He was a doctor, sweetheart. Go on, play, or *we* are going to get worried."

"Don't worry about it, *we* are happy to give us a little privacy. It's only proper."

But she opens her books, hesitates for a few seconds, then smoothes a page with the flat of her hand. "Here! This one's a little sad, in fact really sad, but it's simple and moving, and it shakes the whole musical foundation of its time."

She attacks Mozart's *Rondo in A Minor*. Étienne is instantly swept up in the melody, at once ornate and poignantly melancholic. Bewitched, he moves to stand behind Odile, gazing at the movement of her fingers as they travel across the keys with an agility and precision that fill him with admiration. But in the meeting of hands and keyboard, over and above its parallel black and white components — as if the piano were also deploying expert phalanges — there is something happening that belies the physical effort, transcends the mass of wood and ivory, and leaves the field open for a being made of sound, without density or weight, insubstantial yet more real than the room and its cluster of presences. Between Odile and Étienne, a being suffers the vastness of human suffering, yet the suffering recalls all of childhood's gaiety; the delicate chromatics suggest repressed tears, almost to the point of dizziness, producing a blinding beauty, beauty itself, as tangible as crystal. And suddenly, Étienne remembers a chandelier suspended from a church ceiling, which he once saw cry rainbow tears that instantly resolved into an unbelievably sustained note of wild flame, like a sign to him from heaven. The angel, its dark and golden light, its proof, beyond piety. An angel, powerful as a scream.

"Do you like it?"

He can only answer Odile with a gesture, a hand placed trembling on her shoulder. He fights down a desire to cry, to fall to his knees with joy and admiration. With what can he match this gift, his beloved's gift? How can he repay the blessing that is offered him with open arms?

"I'm listening … deep inside," he says. "You are inside me, the music is inside me. When you play, I live, I listen to myself living."

His cheeks are crimson with the feelings brought on by the grip of sound. Odile gazes at his feverish face, his sparkling eyes and, carried away, embarks on Bach's *Chromatic Fantasy and Fugue*, its incredible lines evoking the splendour of a bundle of

swords. Never has the sublime been manifested in a more vigorous light than in this burst of sovereign beauties, and Étienne is made painfully aware of the ideal beings produced by
human genius of whose company he has been deprived until
now, without even knowing it. Of course he knew that great
music existed, but he'd always believed it was for snobbish con-
cert audiences. It's a real shock to see it springing up — simple,
true, naked — from two adorable arms, from the work of intelligent, nimble hands that are an extension of a heart's feeling,
a heart as large as air and sea, earth and fire, the world!

"You're incredible!" exclaims Étienne after the fugue's
last chords have sounded. "I've never heard a pianist as good
as you are!"

Odile laughs, explaining, "My teacher would really laugh if
she heard you! I've still got a long way to go before I really have
these pieces mastered. It isn't enough to play the notes and follow the composer's instructions. You also have to really think
about the music on your own, and communicate those thoughts.
It takes maturity, a true sensibility, being open to the mysteries
of beauty — the beauty of people, things, everything."

"But what you played had all of that. I've never been so
moved by a piece of music. It's true that, until now, I've never
seen it played, right before my eyes, but I really mean it, I've
never heard anything so beautiful."

"It's because you're discovering a new world, and I'm so, so
happy to be the one who is showing it to you!"

"And what can I do?" says Étienne, a little crestfallen.
"What can I give you in return?"

"Your courage," Odile answers. "Just the beauty of your

courage, your strength, your heart, which is as immense as the air, the blue of the sky!"

She looks at him, still radiating with the magic she has deployed, and Étienne's love leaps toward her incredible grace. For her, he can take on the future and bend it to their will. His hand, with its square fingers, still trembles on her shoulder but it is a gentle trembling, a shiver of flesh that is ready to melt into a caress. Odile tilts her head, catching her lover's hand in a tender trap.

Just then, they hear the front door opening and voices, muffled.

"Papa's here," says Odile, starting to play once more, softly.

Étienne moves back a little, awaiting the lawyer's arrival apprehensively. He soon appears, followed by his spouse. He's a big man, unpleasant, with greying hair. There's something hideous about his dark suit, which shimmers with metallic glints. To Étienne, it seems to make the man a living symbol of riches. It's as if he's clothed in old money, and his jacket and too-big pants whisper like brushed metal. Behind him, his wife's face and impeccable dress display the colours that the dignified man of law is lacking.

"Papa, I'd like to introduce Étienne, my boyfriend."

Mr. Louvier takes the extended hand with visible distaste.

"'Étienne' — I see that you've only got a first name, just like all the kids today."

"Étienne Tourangeau, mister ... sir, excuse me!"

"Oh, you can say 'mister.' 'Sir' has gone out of style, along with everything else ... I like everything to be clear, so before we go any further, I should tell you that I ran into an

182 ~ André Brochu

old friend today, Mr. Lamothe, the lawyer, who knows your charming town quite well since he also lives there. In fact, his neighbour is one of its most respectable and respected citizens, Mr. Garon. You've heard of him, correct? He is a city councillor."

Étienne doesn't turn a hair, though the introduction of this topic is, without a shadow of a doubt, a crushing blow from fate. "I know Mr. Garon," he answers. "Less than two weeks ago, he came to our house and threatened and insulted my mother in a way that was unworthy of a man of integrity."

"A man of integrity! Do you even know what that is? That's pretty good, coming from you, young man! Unfortunately for you, I know all about this affair. I don't know what Mr. Garon's motives were, but his excellent reputation would lead me to think that they weren't without foundation. And since we're on the subject of reputation, I've also heard mention of a family that lives in a big blue house by the water. The house is quite notorious, and, so I hear, has quite a stream of visitors … From what my very good friend Mr. Lamothe suggested when I told him that my daughter was seeing someone by the name of Étienne Tourangeau, it's nothing to crow about!"

"Papa!" Odile intervenes, dismayed by this exchange. "We're not in court, here. Please, I don't want to hear any more of those malicious insinuations."

"What insinuations? I'm only repeating what I've been told, and I'm doing it only because I want to keep you from getting involved with the kind of people that could lead you into God knows what."

"I'm old enough to use my own judgment, and I'm sure there's no truth in what people are saying ... I know the house and the people who live in it, and I can tell you ..."

"Be quiet! You know nothing at all about the facts, or you would never have spoken a single word to a member of the notorious Tourangeau family. The whole world sees the family as the epitome of the worst kind of poverty, happy-go-lucky and loose, physically and morally, in fact, the worst type of social parasites. The mother, Lucie Tourangeau ..."

"That's enough! I'm not going to let you hurl any more insults at the family of the man I love."

"The man you love! Do you even know what love is? You young people are all alike! One twinge of passion justifies any number of stupidities, and you feel entitled to forget everything you've been taught. Frankly, Odile, I'm disappointed in you. I thought you were different, that you could use your brain a little better than that. Until now, you've always behaved like an intelligent girl, you've looked after your future, you've made us proud, you were even thinking about a respectable career and, all at once, it's up in smoke! The young lady is in love. In love with who? With someone who's going to help her achieve her goals, help her to continue to shine in this world? No! Instead, he's a hoodlum, I'm telling you, with a mother who's half squaw, and a father who abandoned his family a long time ago and is the worst kind of bohemian! When I found out about that, I almost had a heart attack!"

"That's exactly what you should have done," retorts Odile, beside herself. "Yes, I love Étienne. He's more important to me than everything in the world. And he's my lover, if you want to know. And he's worth a thousand of you, you and my mother, and your hypocritical respectability!"

"You, the mistress of that piece of trash! A ne'er-do-well who hasn't even finished Cegep and doesn't want to get a job!"

Odile takes Étienne's hand and leads him away, saying, in a terse and final tone, "Goodbye! You'll never see me again!"

"You're not leaving us, you little fool, I'm throwing you out, do you understand? I'm throwing you out! Don't ever set foot here again! Go live with that crazy Tourangeau broad, that's what they call her. Remember that: the crazy Tourangeau!"

Stunned, Étienne lets himself be led into a space of frenzy and disaster, where nothing, not even his Odile, whom he's known only joyous and confident, resembles what he'd hoped for.

26

"It all happened so fast! Are you sure you won't regret this?"

"I should have left a long time ago. My father is incredibly bourgeois. He's gotten rich on legal wheeling and dealing, just like all lawyers, and he tries to forget that by keeping to a rigid moral code. He goes to church every Sunday — honestly — so he's gotten a reputation for being a man of integrity, and probably good cases to defend, too. Catholics take care of each other, especially in a neighbourhood like ours, which still works like a village. I've always hated that kind of double life: completely ruthless in business, and, for the family, completely proper. He's so bad tempered that he convinces himself that he's right. In fact, it's pathetic!"

"But won't your mother miss you?"

"She's abetting him in all this. When he's there, she stays in the background. In any case, I don't think she ever loved me very much. No ... There's just one thing that I'll miss, I guess ..."

"Your piano?"

Her gaze mists over, proof that he was right, but a smile quickly banishes her sadness. "Well, no," she says. "You're worth more to me than everything I'm leaving behind, even Mozart and Bach!"

"I'm going to get a job soon, I promise, and we'll get our own place in Montreal, with a piano, and you'll go on with your lessons."

"My lessons … Poor Mrs. Marin! She'd give me lessons for free, if she knew, but she has so little to live on!"

"We'll be able to get settled by next month. I'm sure there'll be a good opening for me, somewhere."

"What about school? Cegep? Your plans for the future?"

"All in good time. For now, we have to have something to live on."

"I can work. I'll do whatever it takes. I could be a waitress, for example. They get good tips. If we're really careful with our money, you could even go to school."

"I don't want you to sacrifice yourself for me."

He contemplates her. Her face reveals the serious, slight sadness that follows an irrevocable decision and a total lack of anguish about having suddenly cut herself off from her past. The light picks out her face against the masses of summer leaves eddying gently in the evening breeze. They've walked a long way from that unhappy house, hand in hand, absorbing their exile and assessing their chances in a world created for adults and opportunists. The beautiful weather and surrounding tranquility, only slightly disrupted by the indistinct murmur of televisions, lull their forebodings and inspire confidence in the future.

Their steps have taken them near their island, and now they notice it. For them, this is the blessed ground of their union, the place that has forever given each one's body to the other, ordained by joy given and received, created them in the likeness of gods. Pausing before the trembling mass of greenery, from which a blackbird's pure and desolate song emerges, they feel the bite of remembrance and, without a word, decide to return to the palace of ferns and the soft layer of humus and dry leaves where they first revealed their beauty to each other. This time, Odile doesn't hesitate before entering the weak current that hems the half-drowned stones with flame. She moves forward so confidently that Étienne's hold could hinder her, so he lets her go first. She reaches the island and begins to run, laughing, and he runs after her, reaching her just as she lets herself fall on their bed, and devours her with kisses.

When they get up, spent with passion and forced to acknowledge their hunger, the sun is only a cluster of embers on the horizon, and they decide to go home, to Devil's Paintbrush, as quickly as they can. Crossing the train bridge on foot is out of the question, because of Odile, and the thought of paying for tickets when the girl has just had her allowance cut off does not appeal to them. It would be better to take the long way home, using the Saint Eustache bridge a few kilometres away.

"Let's walk to the highway," Étienne suggests, "and then hitchhike."

He puts his left arm around her, and she leans her tired head on him, a little smile occasionally breaking through her daydreams. From time to time, he stops and puts his lips to her face, which is pale with gentle lethargy. "You'll see, sweetheart, everything will work out," he murmurs, to banish dark thoughts.

"With you, I'm not afraid of anything." A tear forms at the corner of her lid, and she crushes it, as if it were a scrap of childhood's foolishness.

On the highway, however, their attempts to find an obliging driver are unrewarded. They give up and are preparing to walk some more when they see an ancient car approaching, its bumpers rattling under the crumpled hood. It pulls up next to them, and a mocking voice heckles them, "If the lady and gentleman would care to climb aboard, they will find their voyage very restful, though hopefully not to eternal rest."

"Gervais?" exclaims Étienne, dumbfounded.

"In person, and at your service. Here, get in the front, the back isn't too clean! That damn Denis can be a real pig when he wants to. Hello, Odile. Give me a kiss." He plants a cavalier kiss on her lips, and she draws back a little.

"I reek of beer," he comments.

"Indeed," says Étienne. "I can smell you from over here. So this is the old Durand that's giving you all that trouble. I thought it got demolished."

"They built them solid in those days."

He takes off with a scream of outraged axles and sets off a burst of honking behind him, to which he responds with an obscene gesture.

"You're driving without a licence?" Étienne points out, after a minute.

"That's obvious, since I don't have one."

"That could cost you."

"I don't have any money, either."

"And that night at the police station? You want to do that again?"

Gervais gives a coarse laugh. "In the end, I might get to like it."

Beside him, Odile lowers her eyes, pretending that she hasn't heard. He laughs again, asking, "Well, are you happy with the limo service? You were at least four kilometres from home."

"What were you doing on this side of the bridge?"

"I like your method of interrogation. Very direct. You'd make a good detective, brother!"

"I'm just trying to make conversation, that's all. Don't tell me then, I don't care."

"No, I'll give you an answer, and a true one, too. For one thing, I wanted to take this fine old machine out for some fresh air — it's so old that standing still means instant rust. And I've been wanting to compare our local beer with the beer they have at that famous tavern on the road to Fabreville. There. Now you know everything. You too, Odile. I've bared my soul and, as you can see, it's as clear as a goldfish bowl."

"After the water's just been changed," suggests Odile, unused to this kind of humour.

"Exactly! There's nothing like a good ride to get some fresh air, or water, as you please. Plus," he adds, with pretended nonchalance, "I didn't want to be around to see it, when *they* started groping each other."

"Hey," interrupts Étienne, sternly, "are you determined to dish dirt?"

"Oh, excuse me! I forgot there was a lady with us. Forgive me, Odile."

"What are you talking about now?" Étienne continues, after a moment.

"Oh, you'll see for yourself, if the bird hasn't flown. That's all the dirt I'm going to dish."

Étienne gets more and more anxious the rest of the way home. Odile's tense bearing tells him that she's being assailed by the memory of that scene with her father, and, one by one, realizing the consequences of her departure. Then he wonders what kind of welcome Lucie will give the young runaway. Bringing Odile into the big blue house can't be done without some upheaval; she and Étienne will be living as man and wife, necessarily displacing Lucie from the room with the big bed. Unless they set up in the veranda until they can find another solution … But what was Gervais talking about just now? Could Lucie have set her cap at a new lover? With the mood she'd been in for the last few days, she's perfectly capable of contracting one of her strategic liaisons, the kind intended to keep misfortune at bay, like that incredible affair with the priest that Fernand witnessed.

Étienne would like to know more, but doesn't dare reopen the matter. Gervais, likely irritated by the remonstrance, won't say another word.

When they get home, Gervais can't hide his astonishment. "Do you recognize that car?" he asks Étienne, in a strange, high-pitched voice.

"That's Garon's car! What's it doing here?"

"When I left, two hours ago, he was just getting here. I couldn't hear the stream of nonsense he started pouring out very well, but it was obvious that they were trying to get rid of us again. And now that we've cleaned up the property, it's to the town's advantage to seize it and sell it."

"You came up with this all by yourself?"

"No, I'm not smart enough. It's Lucie that talked to me about it. She thinks our best protection, the way she put it, was the poor condition of the house. When she saw it all fixed up, she immediately thought we were going to lose it. Thankfully ..."

"What?"

"Thankfully, she has other resources."

Gervais stops speaking. The three of them sit in the parked car, wrestling with their thoughts. Étienne finally breaks the silence.

"What do you mean?"

"If she's been with Garon for two hours, it can only be one of two things: either she's killed him, which is both unlike her and not in her best interest; or she's done the same thing she did to the priest ..."

"And what ..."

Gervais suddenly stretches out his arm and grips Étienne nervously, with no thought for Odile, seated between them.

"There, look! They're coming out together, do you see them? That fat bastard! She's holding his arm affectionately ... Look! Look! He's kissing her, the fat pig. Do you see that?"

It's as if Gervais has seen a ghost. He suddenly starts the car, turns on the lights. Before the others can stop him, he launches the car down the slope at full speed, hurtling toward the grotesque pair, who start to run wildly. The car just misses the councillor, but strikes Lucie dead on, leaving her collapsed absurdly on the hood. Étienne fights with Gervais across Odile, trying to put the brakes on with his hand, but the wheels slide on the bank's wet grass.

27

In the hospital room, cut off from neighbouring beds by a curtain, Étienne is not living, he is surviving, an infinite distance from himself. At each moment, he feels himself tumbling again, everything toppling with him, falling, there is only the endless jolt, the impact of bodies, no sound. A moment between darkness and infinity, an evening moment, rent open. Then the crash and crushing, and the water's mouth, snatching, swallowing. He loses consciousness, comes to, suffocating; they're in the water, floating, Lucie ripped open in front of him, skewered by a hood ornament; Odile, her gaze fixed, her forehead marked with a wound's wide stripe. He wants to open the door, get out and take Odile, but his right foot is broken. He doesn't feel the pain, he just has a hard time moving. He manages to get out with Odile, pulling her out of the car, which, lighter now, starts to drift toward open water. Somehow he swims toward the shore and, his strength gone, gives his precious burden to the first witnesses to reach him. Then he goes down, down, and wakes up here. He does not wake up. The nightmare is here, all around him. The catastrophe continues. They're all dead: Lucie, Gervais, Odile. The priest told him so, the priest who came with words full of God and eternity, his eyes crying.

They're dead, and so is Étienne, though he is still present in the world, in life. For after death, the world and life still exist. He watches them. He watches his white stone foot above his body, suspended in a grotesque, complicated device. A foot, surviving, above his body.

Time is one long sorrow.

He would have wanted to live, he grew up as a child does, in spite of how bad things looked. He grew between Lucie's legs, large Lucie with her insinuating caresses, muddled high-sounding words, surrounded by children who were like a troupe of compensations for her own lonely childhood. He played at growing up, at waiting, then, not long ago, discovered the greatest, most beautiful of games, a game for two whose goal is to make just one, to lose yourself in what you are not, what the other is, what she is. The woman. Odile ... There was Lucie, there is Odile, and neither exists. They are lies told by a mendacious life, he is alone against life, against Odile, against Lucie. He is alone against himself, waiting for the nightmare to end, to fall, for day to fade, for the great death to come and swallow him, just as it swallowed the car of ill-fortune. The car had drifted gently until it reached the abyss, then it sank, went to rest at the very bottom among the box springs and mattresses, old refrigerators, among the living rooms and bedrooms of the river. It was from there, from the very bottom, that they fished up the gutted Lucie and Gervais, whose eyes, in death, sparkled still.

The abyss. Twenty-five metres down, it is completely dark. Twenty-five metres of dark water, made thick by pollution. And it is down there, among the debris, among the refuse fallen from homes, the storehouse of broken dreams, that Étienne wants to go, once he's back on his feet, released into life. It's there that he wants to go, put his arms around the young woman, the woman in bloom, Odile, lost to this life; and there, pressing his mouth to her lips, he also wants to hold, at the same time, the great dirty blessed mother, the one who, from his earliest childhood, bathed him in words full of ardour and absurd happiness and a boundless love that she gave to everyone like a madwoman. In the body of his friend, his lover, he will possess great, savage, motherly Death, who laughs and bleeds, pollutes, condemns her sons to a trivial, failed existence, futureless. A life like the miserable destiny of her broken people, a bouquet of devil's paintbrush crushed, torn, green mud. Perpetually miserable Mohawks. A heap of chimeras, signed Lucie. A people, extinct.

A bed of drifters and dreamers.

about the translator

Alison Newall, born and raised in Montreal, studied literature at McGill University, earning a BA and an MA. She has taught literature and writing, and has been working as a translator, editor, and writer for ten years.